THE FOREVER

PROMISE

ABOUT THE AUTHOR

15 year-old Marcus Tay, aka MarcTay, is a young writer who resides in Virginia. He has previous books including the Lanterncup series and the single The Experiences of Colin Shaker. He aims not just to entertain the general public but also to communicate messages through his patterns of writing. To wrap it up, his goal is to have more and more people of every age to grasp their pencil and a sheet of paper and start jotting down ideas from their heads.

Author: Marcus Tay (15 years old)

Printed in the United States of America

@2019 Tay's Imagination World.

ISBN #: 978-0-9964830-8-7

PART ONE

"Being deeply loved by someone gives you strength, while loving someone deeply gives you courage." –Lao Tzu.

There's something about love not a single soul can comprehend. It is something that keeps the world spinning every day and encourages every action that is to be completed. Love gives birth to feelings, and feelings give birth to emotion. Love breaks all bonds of law and correctness. Love is superior. Love cannot be understood, for it writes history in indirect manners. Impossibility is possibility in love. Love is really only love. Love is love.

And here's the story of love.

Cole Alessandro awoke with a shudder. Brushing back his hair, he rolled the bedsheets away and slipped into his slippers. The clock read 8:30am, which was a usual time he got up out of bed. Cole walked into his bathroom and went through the morning routine: face-washing, teeth-brushing, hair-combing. It was always the same.

He was happy for another day…where he could enjoy more of the joys life brings and the spice and flavor that is sometimes added. Cole finished and sauntered out of the bathroom and towards the couch by the window of his room. Today was a free day and one where he could catch up on rest. Cole reached over his nightstand and picked up his guitar from the guitar-stander that stood adjacent to the bed.

One foot on the leg-rest and the other on the floor, Cole started strumming and singing his favorite pop tunes while observing the world through the window. The sunlight covered half of his face, but it didn't seem to bother him. Cole sang with his heart, and he was a great singer. His voice was as if a dozen doves had sprang from their nests and flew smoothly behind a waterfall. He closed his eyes. Every strum was a heartbeat. Every chord and arpeggio represented a beauty of life. His melody enriched the air around him. His harmony supported the many fragments that longed to be connected into a singular body.

> "Oh oh, I wished you were here with me, how great that we would be, you and I can see, that we really don't have so much we need.
>
> Now come on this journey I'll lead, for we sprouted from small seeds. And then we became two large trees.
>
> So as long as this will go, you are still my key. And because of this, out here I'm free."

Cole was about to move on to the chorus, but then his phone buzzed.

Cole approached his phone and saw the notification. It read: "I love you, wanna have lunch together??" with a smiley emoji. The sender was Hazel Francesca. Cole smiled almost automatically, for they were probably as close as two people can be.

Cole and Hazel texted to each other on most nights for hours because they couldn't sleep, and they always did so in the morning too. Hazel was his girl. They would talk about nearly everything. From the most embarrassing to the most unlikely topic, chances are that they've spoken about it. How it went was that one of them started the conversation and then they just broke off of that initial statement.

And every time it was time to leave, they would write "hey, you're cool, bye forever!" They wouldn't mean it obviously, but this was true. Cole shared drinks with Hazel whenever they were together and they even snuggled against the other once in a while.

Although they were insanely close, Hazel was never announced as Cole's official girlfriend, but Cole probably treated her as. They'd met in third grade, but they were both now fresh out of college, living in the same city together, although separate apartments. They'd even attended the same college. Hazel was the only person he'd told all his secrets and honest opinions toward, while Hazel did the same back. Overall, they were best buddies from the start. Hazel was the one person he'd trusted when everything else let him down. She was a solid cornerstone, the framework of the structure. Hazel, not once, had let him down.

The day they met was a memorable one.

There was a science project with a volcano. The teacher called out all the names of the groupmates in order.

Cole had wanted to be with the popular kid named Bradley, but they weren't put together unfortunately. Instead, he was paired with Hazel Francesca, a really cute, brown-haired girl. But she's a girl, Cole thought with his third grade conception. He quickly shrugged it off. At least she's crazy cute, he resided.

Hazel's eyes were the game-winners. They shone with elegance and possessed the traits of a goddess. However, she was also a really relatable and amiable girl too, which captured Cole's heart. Hazel knew how to make a conversation flow with ease and had humor. Not only that, but she was good at incorporating it at the right time. She made anyone she worked with comfortable even though they were knowing her for the first time. It was like she was a friend to everyone from the beginning. Cole loved her for that. He thought it was out-of-the-world.

They were doing a science lab experiment.

The directions said to drop a mento mint into the volcano to watch it bubble on top, but Cole took a slice of apple from his lunch bag and dropped it in to see what would happen. Others thought he was stupid, but Hazel giggled at his insight.

After that, Hazel approached Cole as they left the class and walked in the hallways for a tad. "You seem different, but in a good way," Hazel had told him. "Yeah, thanks," Cole had replied. "Yeah, nice to meet you, I'll see you around?" Hazel asked. "Oh yea, see you girlie!" Cole responded with some drastic effect.

They parted ways after this, but saw each other again during recess.

Cole and his whole class were strolling to the doors that would lead them outside to the playground and basketball courts with the guidance of a teacher when he forgot his water bottle. He ran to get it back when no one was looking and then came around again. This time he saw Hazel almost stepping on a puddle of water by the water fountain. But he was too late to warn her.

She slipped and slid several feet, her sweatpants all wet.

Cole ran to her and lifted her up, saying "are you okay?"

"Oh hey! It's you! I know you!" Hazel exclaimed.

"You're really nice for helping me, you know," Hazel addressed him. "No, it was just, I had to do that," he smiled back. Hazel poked him in the side of the ribs. "Wanna be besties from now on?" she inquired. "Sure!" Cole seemingly blurted.

That was how they met.

Cole texted back on his phone. "Ok, yea, do you wanna go to that seaside restaurant u love..? I know you can't get enough of that place," he wrote. After a second, a message popped up. "Yeah! Let's do it," Hazel confirmed without hesitation. "See u then," Cole wrote.

He put down his phone and fell onto his bed, feeling happy. Hazel was honestly the best girl ever, he could never ask for more. Neither could Hazel on the other side. They were truly besties4life.

Before the boardwalk came into view, Cole made a momentous decision. He decided to once-and-for-all ask Hazel if they wanted to be together for a long time…like an actual, serious long time (you get what I mean). Cole trotted on the stairs and appeared onto the boardwalk. It was a grand, sunny day. People were either walking or biking, and stores sold souvenirs that read "Welcome to Seattle" or "Seattle's finest," for that was where they lived.

Cole was early, so he took some time wandering around himself. The ocean was as calm as ever today with glimmering and glittering sparkles of sun rays on it. The beach was only partially-occupied; somehow, many people didn't take their time to come today.

Then, he saw her. She was as beautiful as ever.

The wind blew her hair, hiding a section of her face. Hazel's eyes glistened. Her features were outstanding, and the setting made her look the best she ever was. Cole's consciousness dropped at her sight. She was very dazzling and cool and spontaneous and cute…he didn't know. Anyway, he always looked forward to seeing her even after they've seen each other for quite a while always.

"Hey Cole…" Hazel started as she waved at him through the masses of people moving past her. "Hey Hazel…" Cole trudged toward her as he avoided people walking past him.

They immediately grasped each other's hands. "Boardwalk fries?" Hazel asked. "I'm hungry," she stated.

"Bet, let's go…" Cole agreed.

There they went, hand-in-hand, up the boardwalk. They approached a food stand that sold burgers, shakes, and of course, fries. There was a decent line, so they stopped.

"One basket of boardwalk fries with chili peppers and nacho cheese please," Hazel ordered with her gentle voice. The cashier went to make their food and then returned with a basket the size of a bucket. Cole payed, and they headed off from there.

"I just love the ocean, it's the best. You can hear the wind, you can see the water, and you can feel the sand. It's heaven. The ocean is heaven," Hazel said.

"Hey, that reminds me…ocean time? I mean that's what we came for," Cole proposed. Hazel responded, "I guess so. Whatever you want," she smiled sweetly. "We're both here for a good time, not a long time," she added. "Wait, how do u know that?" Cole questioned suspiciously. "What? You thought I didn't know?" Hazel punched Cole's shoulder playfully. "My bad senorita Hazel," Cole answered with a Spanish accent, hiding a successive grin.

They descended wooden stairs onto the beach and Hazel ran to the sea. She soaked her feet instantly and started splashing around. Hazel called his name, urging him to go and have some fun. Cole went after her and they both splashed each other in the shallow water.

There, Cole and Hazel sprayed water on each other and played tag. They raced and raced until they couldn't move anymore. "You're slow," Hazel taunted. "You're so fast," Cole replied sarcastically.

Then, as the sun started to lose its power through mid-afternoon, they had had enough and ventured onto the sand. Cole wrapped a towel around himself and Hazel and they sat for several minutes.

"I really liked today, it was great having you here…" Hazel said as she watched the horizon.

"Yeah, same here. You really make my day up. Without you, I don't know, it just wouldn't be as *swell,*" Cole agreed. They both used the word "swell" every time they wanted to say something that was overly great or just better in general. It was part of their communication.

"Hey, if we ever are separated for some reason, remember this. We will forever belong to each other and you're my home and I'm yours too," Hazel brought up.

"Ok," Cole nodded.

"Are you being honest that you really believe that?" Hazel asked in a somehow investigative tone.

"Oh yea, you bet I am," Cole replied.

"Ok, I believe you then," Hazel concluded.

They sat in silence for several moments afterward.

"Sunsets are when the sea goes calm, and colors streak the pre-night sky, where the seagull flies until the sky faints dark." Hazel spoke this with a sense of rest, like rest was finally here.

Cole pondered this. It was sure a meaningful quote, at least it sounded like one.

"Let's make a list of the things that we do that is different than what we do with other people," Hazel proposed. "I'll start," Cole said.

"We say "swell" a lot, we have certain habits, we know a lot about each other, basically everything," Cole spoke. "Yeah, you're right, I guess we're so close maybe we're one person instead of two, you know," Hazel pointed out. "Maybe, I think," Cole responded.

"Hey, you should go surfing, I want to see you do it," Hazel introduced the idea. Cole said yes and he went to rent a surfboard and brought it back. "See you Cold Cole!" Hazel joked.

Cole got onto his surfboard and paddled into the water.

He stood up and surfed several waves. Cole looked back to the beach and he could see Hazel sitting there watching him. Her smile, her face, her voice, he will never forget any of it.

Cole saw a big, thick wave coming. He was prepared. Cole whipped around a smaller one so he went vertical to its side. He rushed into the wave through a crest. The sunlight shone through the water as it flowed over his head. He felt the water with one hand as the other maintained balance. Cole was nearing the end of the tunnel.

He could feel that everything felt so good. In fact, too good. Through the tunnel of water, he could see images and flashes of his life inside the water as though they were pictures. Cole thought he was going to heaven and strove to get to the other side. He zipped out of the wave and then everything disappeared and reappeared.

Except it didn't reappear exactly as it was before. No beach. No water. Nothing. He was lying on the ground somewhere. Cole stood up and found himself in a meadow of yellow grass.

What was going on? Where am I? What just happened?

Cole didn't know.

"Hazel?" Cole cried. "Hazel?" There was no sign of her. He ran around the meadow but couldn't find a single other person. He broke down and collapsed on the grass. Hazel was gone, nowhere to be found. Why? How? Where am I?

There was no one to consult nor any explanations. For now, he was on his own, and that was all.

It was 2am with the morning dew starting to reside. Cole sat teary as his back was against a tree trunk. The wort part was that he didn't know where he was and how this occurred. It was as bemusing as to the situation itself, but all he knew was that he had to get back to that beach before anything else.

But where to start?

Cole rose and staggered across the meadows towards a cliff-top. As he got to the edge, in the distance, there was an entire metropolitan area characterized by a vast flashing of lights from skyscrapers and the city skyline itself being so colorful.

At least he was close to human civilization though.

Before he turned to somehow get to the city, a sudden thought rampaged through his brain. His eyebrows contracted against each other. Whipping and lashing around, Cole swiftly adjusted his eyes to study the city building placement.

It couldn't be, no absolute way. Seattle sat smack right in front of his eyes and he felt embarrassed for not recognizing it after living there for nearly his entire life so far.

Seattle? That meant whatever took him away from the beach and then blasted him into that meadow couldn't have taken him that far away. Cole was overjoyed by this, and it drove his motivation.

He was eager to get to Hazel's house and then surprise her. He wanted to tell her about what happened and if she knew anything about it, but right now it was time to get out of there.

Picking through the woods, Cole recognized that he was in Olympic National Park, the most profane park in Washington State. He always adored nature and its many aspects. It surely was a place for quiet reflection and peace.

Cole made it to an unpaved gravel road and followed it in the direction of the city. Several deer walked by and he admired the beauty of their brown spots. Cole eventually made progress in miles, all while thinking of the past and also the many futuristic possibilities that could enhance the excitement in his life. He smiled at this, it kept him eager to continue and move on with pretty much everything, and especially, to move on with Hazel.

By 4am he had gotten to a gas station where he decided to buy several bag of chips to have an early morning celebration with Hazel in her living room. Walking past the doors, he heard music from atop and gazed into the different sections and aisles.

Hazel lived in a bungalow-styled home just outside the most urban places in the city. From time to time, Cole would head over every time she invited him to have some fun. They would have sleepovers, pillow fights, hide and seek games, and many more. It was their happy place together. But most of the time, even when they weren't even sure of how to spend their weekends, they just did whatever and enjoyed each other's comfort. Hazel and Cole were besties in the extreme end.

Cole found an abandoned bike and took it. He hopped on and started peddling down the roadway that would take him to her house. Occasionally, a car would pass by with a whoosh! The morning air flew through the gaps in his stiff but cushioned hair. In the distance, the sun was creeping out of a mountain, halfway out. It was the start of sunrise.

Cole crossed a river and made it into the suburbs. He sped past marketplaces and houses, swinging around traffic to avoid cars and beating traffic lights. Coming up, there was an entrance to a neighborhood that had a stone-brick wall with the words read in brass: "Royal Plains."

He couldn't wait. Cole went up a curb and onto the sidewalk, rushing past dozens of houses and turning blocks. At last, he'd made it to a house that didn't really stand out as much as many other houses were in the same neighborhood. However, this house was different because it was a special location. It was one of the locations Cole would always come back to and relive good memories.

Cole parked his bike and walked about the stairs to the front door. He did the standard "3 knock" that he'd established with Hazel as a secret code kinda thing that they only knew.

No reply.

3 more knocks. But again, no door opening.

Finally, Cole rang the bell, growing impatient.

Hazel twisted the handle and pulled the door open, revealing herself. She was in a bathrobe with her hair, still wet, draping down to her shoulders. Cole's heart immediately sank at her features and how sharp she looked there. But still, this was always.

"Hey, how's it ..." Cole lifted a foot to step in.

"Excuse me! Who are you? And why are you trying to come in?" Hazel said in her controlled tone. Cole always love this virtue of Hazel. Although when most people would go one way, she went the other. Hazel was always open to the slightest possibility of any misunderstanding or unexpected, impossible reason for an action.

If it was for others, they would have struggled with Cole and kick him out of their house already. But instead, she didn't.

Cole was intrigued at this statement. "What do you mean, c'mon are you playing me right now?" Hazel shook her head, and the truth was, she wasn't kidding from her expression.

Cole was puzzled. "Are you okay? Or are you just a very good actresses because I know you are…"

"I don't even know you… who are you?" Hazel asked, staring straight into his eyes, demanding an answer.

"I am Cole! Your …" he was about to say boyfriend but then caught himself because they weren't really official yet. "I am your bestie," he concluded. "Your boy."

"Listen, I'm not sure who you are and why you're calling me your bestie essentially, but if you want to talk about it, I mean, although it's kinda early to have strangers in your house, you might as well come in and we can talk about this … because I bet I'm as clueless as you are now…" Hazel grinned at the last part.

"Yeah, but I'm not a stranger, I told you, I know you, maybe a little too much sometimes, but that doesn't matter," Cole argued.

"Well, if you don't want to come in, that's up to you," Hazel said, putting her hand on the door and about to close it.

"NO! I mean fine. Ok. Whatever. Sure. I'll come in," Cole said.

She was so freaking chill, but at the same time, why is she denying that she knows him?

Who lets an unknown person enter their residence so easily? Cole tensed and relaxed, careful of his every move. He didn't want to appear awkward or dangerous or even suspicious.

So lastly, with a straight face, Cole shouldered his way inside while in the process, accidentally bumping Hazel (because that's what they always did before). Hazel reacted with surprise, but even so, Cole could see a glint of familiarity in her eyes which prompted him to ponder on what exactly happened at the beach.

Could he have been possibly engulfed by the gigantic wave and died instantly from water pressure? That would explain waking up somewhere different and Hazel not recognizing him.

But what? If this was in fact heaven, was it true that heaven was a mere copy of earth in terms of layout and lives but also simply lost relationships?

Sure Hazel was welcoming, but she was also alert at the same time, watching every expression of Cole's. It was like she was trying to read him and figure out what his deal was.

Cole noticed this and assured her, "I'm just here to get answers to..." he trailed off, unsure of how to explain what had occurred. "It might seem strange but ...you gotta believe me when I ..." he shook his head, unsure of how to continue.

"Hey," Hazel spoke in her comforting, soft voice, "Come in first then sit down, that had help," she motioned.

Cole made sure to not make such a big scene when the feeling of a warm, watery tongue licked his ankle. He jumped spontaneously without second thought.

Looking down, there was a bichon frise staring up at him with intent, dark-colored eyes. When did Hazel get a puppy?

"Oh yeah, this is Archie. Archie, Cole. Cole, Archie. There we go! I've always loved introducing two people I know," Hazel said dreamily. "Yeah, I remember that time when you had to introduce Tyler the Turtle to me, the one that kept rolling around your backyard, like literally rolling around in his shell," Cole brought up. "Wait how did you know that," Hazel squeezed her eyes, curious. "Oh right, I didn't explain yet..." Cole said, and he headed towards the couch after petting Archie.

Her living room totally portrayed her personality.

"I remember this place," Cole muttered. He could see the bright yellow walls with brown furniture to settle down the tone so it wouldn't be too lively (exactly who she was). He recalled all the times they had there: solving puzzles, binge-watching, just normal talking.

Thinking of all this, Cole broke into a smile.

Hazel decided to sit on the chair to his left while Cole occupied the three-person couch.

Cole went down to business. "So you and I are like best buddies. We do everything together including … I'd rather not say. But yes. Uh, the last time we were together was on a beach … it was sunny and really hot. There were a lot of people outside that day. Then I went surfing while you watched me from the beach and I saw a "big one" coming. So I whooshed around the front and went in the side. But then, when I returned out the other side, I appeared in a meadow without a surfboard or my swimming trunks. Instead, I was dressed in my normal causal clothes, jeans and a t-shirt, and …wait a minute, what's the date today?"

Hazel took her phone out of her pocket. "May 15th 2020."

Cole hadn't bothered to check the date that was before he had appeared in the meadow. It could have quite possibly been the same day but he was positive both realities were of the same month in the same year, so probably not much would have changed.

He immediately regret not knowing a crucial part of information.

Hazel could see his frustration on his countenance. That was one of the gifts Cole admired about Hazel; she could identify someone was going through a hard time just by watching them.

"Hey, its fine, whatever you said happened probably happened for a reason... or at least something. Nothing happens without a reason... I learned that a long time ago," Hazel got up and sat on the couch too, right next to him.

Cole looked up at her and their eyes met briefly. "Did anything I just said have anything to do with you...?" Cole asked on the verge of tears. Hazel pondered. "Sadly no. But I'll help you try to get this whole thing pieced out so it would make sense. Promise."

Cole was incredulous. "You would sacrifice time to help someone you don't even know who claims that he knows you and recounts a story that obviously is not even in your memory..."

And that one word response forever changed Cole's view of Hazel.

Most girls would say "of course" or "why not" or even "sure" but there was something different about Hazel.

She said definitively "yes."

26

The audacity in this, the lack of hesitation was so grandeur!

"Ok thank u," Cole replied, feeling as though he had been blow off to space by himself.

"Well, I've got time the rest of the month so care to join me? There's a whole bucket list of fun adventures we could go through and you look like a lost boy, plus u ARE kinda cute no lie, so u want to do this?" Hazel seemingly just asked out-of-the-blue.

Cole glanced at her, for she was looking expectant. Hazel didn't even know her, but he guessed that she trusted him and wanted to know more about him. He was beginning to doubt that he was the only one that knew all the experiences they had shared before the incident occurred but somehow, even when Hazel didn't know any of this, she had a feeling that was so powerful it broke through every barrier or boundary.

"Hey, you should get some rest, we're gonna do a lot today," Hazel exclaimed excitedly. Cole seemed lost at words. "Yea, there's a room upstairs that has never been used. Be my guest, be the first to sleep there. And I'll tell Archie to be there with you."

"You're honestly so amazing," Cole couldn't help it.

"Thank me later, we've got plans to accomplish…" Hazel pointed at him and drooped her head in a playful fashion.

Hazel was a blessing, a beautiful human being in and out. Cole didn't know how to act so he got up and went to the stairs. As he trudged up, he kept wondering about everything. Cole reached the landing and found a room that had blue walls…it seemed like the one she was talking about so he entered it.

Inside was a bed with curtains draped around the windows and a desk. There was an entire CD Record Collection so as materials for writing and coloring, notebooks, and many pictures and artifacts from the beach including conch shells. But what caught Cole's eyes the most was the guitar that stood on its stand in the corner next to the sun-lit window. It was a mahogany-wood acoustic.

He wasn't going to sleep for the next few hours before Hazel would wake him up to start "their plans," for he was going to recite some songs he remembered.

Closing the door, he picked up the guitar and sat down on the bed. Then, with a single strum, he started singing and plucking the guitar. For minutes this went, and then hours.

It was getting brighter and brighter, and Cole was singing in his sweet, manly voice while attaching his combination of improvisation, chords, and melody together.

There was a knock on the door finally. Cole stopped and opened the door, revealing Hazel.

"I love your voice," Hazel spoke nervously, glancing at Cole for a split second but then looking away. "Your playing also sounds good," and again, she was batting her eyes and moving her tongue around her mouth, playing the polite girl.

Cole sneaked a smile. "Well come on in, let's sing together. Do you know these songs?"

Hazel finally gained her confidence. "Of course dude!" she grinned devilishly. "What do you think I am huh...someone who doesn't listen to music ..?" she demanded. Cole tilted his head to one side and shrugged. "You seem like the unpredictable type so I mean …who knows??" "Oh come on, keep playing," Hazel shot back flirtingly.

So Cole resumed with his guitar playing and singing. He sang the same song as he had before that day… before the mysterious incident that had severed their relationship.

"Oh oh, I wished you were here with me, how great that we would be, you and I can see, that we really don't have so much we need.

Now come on this journey I'll lead, for we sprouted from small seeds. And then we became two large trees.

So as long as this will go, you are still my key. And because of this, out here I'm free."

They both sang at the top of their lungs, and Cole realized how good of a singer Hazel was too. Before, Cole knew she had always had a genuine interest in music, but she never demonstrated her talent. This was the first time she was actually singing in front of him.

Cole could always remember her humming, but this was different.

So powerful was this that they had even kept singing as they were in the car on a small, country road going to a place Hazel deemed, "Very pretty." They had left Seattle altogether and driven down south, somewhere along the seaside but not too close in a hilly area.

On one side were the mountains and the plains while on the other side, there was the ocean. They were on top of high cliffs and rocky shores where the waves broke endlessly. It was a cloudless, seemingly perfect day to be out and enjoy the wonders of life.

At last they were tired and couldn't sing anymore. Cole was driving Hazel's small five-person sedan that could lose the top and that's exactly what they did.

Hazel gave out a sigh of happiness and relief.

"It's so nice, days like this one," she told Cole as she stared in front of her at the two-lane highway, one going in each direction.

"You know, it's nice to go somewhere once in a while and forget about everything," Cole pointed out. "That's honestly so true. But you're wrong at one thing. Not everything, but everything except the other person…yea," Hazel corrected. Cole knew she was talking about him, but all he did was nod.

They rode in silence for a little bit.

Hazel yawned. "I'm tired," she complained in a sarcastic way. "Already? C'mon we're having the time of our lives …you know me and you together …makes a lot of difference," Cole cheeked a flashing smile.

Hazel stared at him for three full seconds before she sighed and then lied down, her head on Cole's lap. "Although this is dangerous, I'll still let you do it because …" he struggled to find the words … "because you probably can't even say no? Yeah, I can read your mind," Hazel finished. "You're a G!" Cole shot back.

Hazel did her freaking cute act of lifting one shoulder while bowing her head to the side that corresponded to the same arm, all the while blushing. "Of course, what'd you expect?"

"I'd expect a girl who would push me away for every single thing I say," Cole responded honestly. Hazel looked at him with the same glint in her eyes that meant she was puzzled. "What does that even mean?" Hazel questioned. "You know what? I'm not sure," Cole confessed.

"Ok, fine, but now on, you have to listen to me. So when I tell you to do something, I mean, you better do it or else ..." Hazel started. "Woah woah woah," Cole interrupted, "so after ...hey you can't do that!" He protested.

Hazel laughed. "Sure I can, I can do whatever I want boy. I'm too powerful now, and I'm like better than you so ...yeah. That's why." "Noooo, this isn't fair," Cole replied playfully.

"Then correct yourself," Hazel demanded.

"Ok but first, what would you do if I refused to listen to you instead?" Cole challenged as he steered to the left lane.

Hazel thought for a bit. "I would leave you." She lingered longer to see his reaction with a rather malicious sneer.

"That's something ..." Cole acknowledged. "Fine, my apologies. I don't want a girl who is going to *rule* me, just one that I respect. There. You happy now?"

"Happier than ever. By the way, I think you're running out of gas, and plus I need to use the bathroom. No wait, there's a great scenery over there! Let's stop for a moment. C'mon!"

Hazel started tugging on Cole's arm. Cole was forced to stop, because if he didn't stop, he may as well have hit a car on the opposite lane. So he did so maneuvering and slowed down on a gravel-paved side of the road. Hazel jumped out of the car eagerly.

"Isn't that view nice? Like really," she brushed her hand out towards the cliffs and the Pacific Ocean. They were standing on top of a field that led right to the cliffs.

Hazel took Cole's hand and pulled him towards the cliffs. Just feeling her hand brought back previous memories and he zoned out for a second. Cole must have stopped for more than a second because Hazel looked back at him apprehensively.

"You good," Hazel asked, concerned. "Oh sorry, yea, I'm good." He didn't want to bring about the same topic of how he mysteriously woke up in this extremely-close copy of the reality he'd always known for fears of destroying the sensuality of the moment.

Hazel didn't quite believe it but she let it pass. She probably could've guessed what the problem was. However, she had the same thoughts as Cole and they both knew they didn't want to ruin everything.

Hazel took a seat at the cliff and patted the ground next to her for Cole to sit down with her. He sat down and Hazel nested her head on his shoulder. She smelled so good.

"Hey," Hazel said.

"Hey," Cole answered.

They held eye contact for a while, Hazel looking up at him and Cole looking down at her. He could feel a connection, a strong one.

For 20 minutes they enjoyed each other's company.

"I love this life. I like doing this. Just sitting here and watching what's around …it's incredible," Hazel pointed out.

"Same. I really love it too. It's relaxing," Cole agreed.

After a while, Hazel said, "Let's go."

So they made their way back through the low-grass field dotted with occasional dandelions, towards the car.

Then they went on their way. "It should be here. I've always loved this place …somewhere to the right next to the ocean," Hazel explained. "I used to come here with my family."

"It's like a free-for-all place that's super peaceful. It's like a place with so much greenery and a white building in the middle. There's also gigantic white curtains that flap around every time there's wind," Hazel added. "And plus, there's a piano there. You can play by the seaside."

"I can't wait," Cole admitted.

Cole entered onto a long road with plains on both sides and rectangular bushes. He could see a white building in the middle surrounded with greenery that was undoubtedly maintained.

"Just park on the side ... there aren't any parking spots, it's alright," Hazel told him. "'K," Cole replied.

They got out of the car and Hazel led the way towards the white building in the center. "There aren't any entrances, you have to brush back one of those gigantic curtains to get in."

She took ahold of one of the curtains and pulled it back and disappeared through. Cole was next. He took ahold of the same white curtain that was like 15 feet high and really wide and then moved around it into the building.

Since they were still technically outside, there wasn't any air conditioning but rather the wind. The curtains swayed around and around. Between each white pillar was a curtain. The ground was marble and the roof was flat and stucco. There was nothing else inside (no table, no chairs, no nothing).

Except for a main rectangular, empty area, there was another one of these that sat perpendicular to the one they were in right now. It pointed in the direction of the ocean and was attached to this one. And in the other room was a grand piano with its top opened up.

Cole used to play the piano, and he could still remember several Mozart sonatas and also some from the Romantic Era.

He strode toward the piano bench and adjusted it. Then, with careful hands, he sat down and placed his fingers on the keys. As though it was magic, the music poured out of him.

Cole wasn't in control of his hands anymore. His muscles were independent. They made the fingers fly all across the piano keyboard. They jumped, played chords, and made melodies.

Cole didn't realize he was closing his eyes as he played. Not just that, his body was swaying from side to side with an exaggerated motion every time it was urged to go the other way.

Finally, when he opened his eyes, he could sense somebody right next to him so he sneaked a swift look. It was Hazel, on the marble, white ground with her knees tucked to her chest.

"So I'm guessing you liked it?" Cole teased. "I didn't like it, I *adored* it, Hazel corrected quickly. "Well, your turn though. I'm done here," Cole stood up and lifted his hands to show that he indeed had enough.

"C'mon you have to be like that? I really thought you were the nice guy bro ..." Hazel gave him a look of dismay.

"You know what? You should actually go down to LA and become an actress because ..." Cole started. "Because what? You think I'm good? Aw that's so nice of you! But no," Hazel turned down. "What? Why? Doesn't everyone want to be on the screens?" Cole asked. "It's not that. I'd be a great opportunity but it's just not who I am," Hazel answered.

"I mean right now, since we're both already out of college we should be finding a job together but that's alright. We're at that stage where we don't really have any income so I'm just living off what I have right now: the car, my house ...but I know sooner or later I may need to find one fast and stop living off what my parents provide for me," Hazel said.

"That's true. Me too. I'm a studio architect though, if you didn't already know. I just started like a month ago. So far so good," Cole explained to her. "Wow, that's awesome! I wish I had a job, but I'll try to find one," Hazel responded. "Yeah, you majored in marketing in college …that'd get you somewhere with ease," Cole said. Hazel suddenly seemed surprised.

"How'd you know that?" she asked.

Cole knew he should've just kept his mouth shut.

"Oh right, yea, about that," Cole stuttered. "It was how I knew about you in the first place, like the "weird thing," he continued. Hazel clearly wanted to help him out so she added, "Ok, remember how I promised to help you? Let's talk."

"Just a side thought, we should've brought Archie. But whatever. So let's start with this, since I minored in counseling, I'll ask you this first. Was there anything you were certain about that led up to the event or happened after it occurred," she suggested.

"Not really. I told you about it earlier. I was in a wave and then got out the other side only to realize the ocean and the beach were gone replaced by a meadow of tall grass and occasional flowers in Olympic National Park. It's like I woke up in a separate dimension, one parallel to the one I was in except we don't know each other, that's the only difference. I'm not sure about other people...when we get back to the city I can see but for the time being, yeah, this is the only difference," Cole ranted.

"Dude that's wild. Crazy maybe. But I like it, and I do certainly believe you ...actually," Hazel replied. "Thanks for being so *understanding,* not a lot of people are like you. You're just different and that's why I fell in ..." Cole halted right there. "Love?" Hazel completed the sentence. "Love? That's why you fell in love with me?"

Cole made no attempt in hiding it. "Yeah, you're definitely right."

Hazel nodded and looked elsewhere at the corner of the room. Cole could see a flicker and twinkle in her eye followed by a beam she tried to suppress but wasn't successful at doing.

"Yeah, I think I really do love you too," Hazel said out-of-the-blue. "Even though I don't know you and you claim that I know you …given everything that has happened today …you and me, we took it pretty easy yet we could relate to each other. That's what a girl wants."

Cole couldn't suppress his laughter. "What can I say? Me too."

"You may figure out one day what really happened on your beach day but for now, play me some more songs please," Hazel begged.

Cole practically skipped over to the piano where his hands flew once again across the keyboard. The sound of the piano rang across the building, and across the fields, and across the Pacific, hopeful to reach the other side. Hazel sat and listened to the music, charmed. Cole played straight from his memory and the tunes flowed out of him like a bucket of water being poured out into a large canister.

There they were one moment, and there they weren't the other moment. Once you could see them, the next you couldn't. The wind blew through every curtain and caused

42

them to sway in and out. Sometimes, the curtains concealed them inside, sometimes they didn't. It was all a matter of nature's choices and its elements.

The sun passed through during the day from high above. Sometimes, the sun rays were hidden behind the clouds, sometimes they weren't. Slowly, the color of the sky turned from light blue to dark blue. And even more slowly, the sun made an arch in the sky and started descending down towards the omnipresent horizon.

Cole and Hazel laid on the hood of their car which they re-parked next to another cliff by the sea. Only one other older couple had visited the place during the day but were long gone. They lay there next to each other watching the stars.

"Hey do you know the constellations?" Cole asked her.

Cole thought he knew everything about Hazel, but it'd never occurred to him that she knew little to nothing about constellations or rather space in general. "Not really. I know there's something called a "Big" and "Little Dipper, though," Hazel replied.

"Yes, but there's also Aquila, Sagittarius, Capricorn, Scorpius, and a whole lot of other ones. See?" Cole pointed and traced his finger, doing connect-the-dots.

"Which one? You're not being clear... it's like you're pointing to that one when you mean the other one ...I'm confused," Hazel replied, pointing her own finger out to explain.

"Ok, I'll do my best, but no complaints," Cole warned her.

He tried again, drawing out Aquila. "There, you see it now?"

"Uh, I think so. Let me try." Hazel stretched her arm out and traced a finger around several dots (stars). "Yeah except, you don't go around them, you go through them..." Cole interrupted. "Hey! I was concentrating," Hazel complained, giggling. "Woah there! Sorry girl. Didn't mean to offend you," Cole reacted in his gentleman manner.

"You're not cool, you know that? Yet I still like you because you're so cute all the time," Hazel pinched his arm. "You've only known me for a day!" Cole responded. "Yeah, but you're the type that's so *affable* to like in a day," she corrected herself. "Remind me cuz

my vocab is bad. What does affable mean?"
Cole inquired. Hazel slapped her face and
shook her head. "You're kidding right? You're
what ... a studio architect and you don't know
what affable means? Are you even social? It
means friendly." Cole replied, "Don't blame
me! Studio architects don't need to know this
stuff."

It was only almost a day and Cole had
already fallen in love with the same girl twice.

Hazel snuggled in closer to him by
pulling his arm towards her and scooting
several inches.

"You're really *comfortable.* Like you're a
nice pillow, I don't know," Hazel pointed out.
"Is that supposed to be a compliment girl?"
Cole readily asked. "Of course!" Hazel replied.

She started poking him and he
scrambled, almost falling off the hood. "Don't
make me taser you," Cole warned.

"Make me," Hazel challenged. "Ok, you
asked for it," Cole concluded.

He started tasering Hazel and she was
laughing so hard that she indeed fell off the

hood. Cole hopped off and picked her up saying, "I'm so so sorry," while smiling also.

There they sat against the wheel, staring up at the sky and having occasional laughing outbursts.

"Good day. I loved it. We should do it more," Hazel suggested.

"Oh yea, that'd be great," Cole said.

"So, I'm throwing a rooftop party tomorrow. I rented one of those spacious high stories in the city, care to join tomorrow night? For the time being, you can stay at my house, that'd help you recover from whatever you said happened," Hazel told him. "Like basically 20 people I know are coming and it would be fun, plus I want to introduce you, my new ...uh... (she didn't know to say boyfriend or not) so she resided with ...friend." "I'm down," Cole replied almost immediately.

"Yeah there's going to be a large glass balcony and a lot of food and a great view of the city," Hazel informed him. "So you don't want to miss it." "How am I going to miss it if you're going to be *yelling* at me to go anyway?" Cole asked curiously.

"Good question. I AM going to force you to go anyway but still keep in mind to go before I do that. You don't want to see me angry," Hazel said. "The Hazel I know never gets angry, or barely at least," Cole pointed out. "Oh yeah? Then I'll prove you wrong." "Oh then please don't," Cole begged earnestly.

She grinned maliciously. "Fine. That's how it is. I don't object," she cried magnificently.

Cole nodded with his lips pressed in an exaggerated motion.

"Do you want to drive home? I'm really tired," Hazel asked him.

"Oh now you want me to do you a favor?" Cole asked.

Hazel laughed. "Who said I couldn't? After all, I'm the princess."

Cole answered, "Ok then Ms. Princess Francesca."

"Also, this Sunday, you should come to my church, we're having a special event," Hazel suddenly brought up. Cole always knew Hazel was a very devout Christian while he wasn't so much of one. She grew up in a Christian household and her parents brought her to church almost every Sunday with the exception of vacations. Hazel knew practically every Bible story by heart while Cole knew one ... Noah's Ark, that's it.

He'd heard it when he was in a bookstore and they were hosting a special occasion called the "Story-Time-A-Thon." Driven by the expressed interests of the children crowding around an adult who was recounting the story of Noah's Ark, he listened intently and watched the reader stop after every page to flip around the book detailed with pictures on it. The children on the ground would express their happiness while the reader continued with the story on her chair.

"That reminds me, can you get the Bible in the car. It's under the driver's seat," Hazel asked him. Cole opened the driver's door and reached under the seat, feeling a book. He pulled it out.

The book was a small version of it, and it was brown. Hazel's grandfather had given it to her before he passed away and she had always cherished it and read it occasionally. Cole sometimes asked her if she would like to go out one day but she would be like she couldn't because she needed to "finish her chapters."

Cole had always seen her read it, but this was the first time she wanted to share it with him.

"And then next Monday, we should go to my cabin that I used to go to a lot. It's really nice there. There's a lake and mountains, and it's secluded in the valley. I'd really like to show you. We've got a lot to do man," Hazel said as she flipped through Bible pages.

"It's a small book with a lot of words," Cole observed. "Yes, it's the word of God, what'd you expect?" Hazel asked of him.

"Let's read this one," Hazel exclaimed as she stopped flipping.

Cole read the title at the top of the passage she was pointing to. "It's about some lost sheep right, that's what it said." "Yes, read on," Hazel urged him, so he continued to read the excerpt.

"Oh ok, so there's 100 sheep, one got lost, and then the shepherd looked everywhere and then when he finally found it, he was overjoyed …I get it! But is that it? I always feel like there is a deeper meaning in these stories," Cole asked her.

Hazel took out a flashlight because it was getting dark and harder to read the words. "Yeah, but imagine you were that lost sheep. If you decide to run away one day or got lost but then your owner found you, wouldn't they be happy?" Cole thought of this. "True, they would probably, unless the shepherd was a big guy which I hope isn't." Hazel elaborated, "Yeah so God is the shepherd, you're the sheep. When he finds you, he's overjoyed at the prospect even though you ran away. He wouldn't be angry or anything, just happy he has found you." "Oh ok…" Cole responded.

"Alright," she closed the Bible and set it inside her car through the open window. They sat there for a while listening to the sound of the waves crashing the shores or the cliffs.

"So if one day you're lost or I'm lost, we would still find each other tirelessly and when we really do, be so happy that I don't know, we're just completely overwhelmed," Hazel related.

"Yeah, I can see that. I can feel that," Cole assured her.

"You're one loveable guy man, I love it," Hazel exclaimed. "And you're one even more loveable girl, I double love it," Cole answered, flashing a smile at her.

"You're so good at talking too. It's like you're charming me into loving you or something. I think I need to break out of the spell. It's about time boy, for holding me captive. Let me go! Or I'll have to try to escape and break your heart. I know you don't want that." Hazel pushed him gently. "No you got it wrong. You're the one that's actually casting the spell. That's why I like you so much," Cole corrected her.

"Maybe. Yeah, I'm the one casting the spell," Hazel admitted.

"That's right princess," Cole said.

"If it's between that random guy and the princess who has got powers…I'd say it's the princess," Cole reasoned. "No way, I think it's obviously the other way around. Ever heard of the least expected having the powers instead?" Hazel brought up.

"Sure, but not in this case though," Cole nodded.

"Whatever, just speaking to you is a waste of time," Hazel announced. "Oh! Is it really?" Cole asked promptly. "I'm not talking to you, you're so annoying and confusing and terrible and all the negative things ..." she made a show of looking away and pushing him aside. "Now I'm getting rejected? Wow, you're such a great girl," Cole smiled again, enjoying his teasing. "Ugh, I can't stand you," Hazel cried. "I hate you but I like you so much at the same time. I want to punch you. I want to get away from you but I want to stay close to you and be with you ...dang it," Hazel ranted. "Not my fault, that's just who I am," Cole defended.

"You're obviously putting me under some sort of spell. Release me!" she rolled her eyes.

"No way, I can't lose something as precious as you ..." Cole spoke.

"You know what? I guess we were just made for each other," Hazel concluded with confidence.

"I second that," Cole corroborated.

Hazel sighed. "Nice conversation." Whenever Hazel uses "nice" instead of "good" that means whatever she is talking about has an extra level of spice to it.

"I think we like each other too much …let's go home and forget about all this. It's like we both lost our minds. We've got more serious things to be thinking about." Hazel demanded.

"You're not even serious when you're talking about being serious," Cole observed.

Hazel eyed him wearily and there was a glowing effect to it.

"I love you so freaking much …"

"Love you too!" Cole blew a kiss at her.

"See you later!" he added.

"You should be an actor, you're really good at it," Hazel told him.

"You should be an actress, you're really good at it," Cole mimicked in Hazel's voice.

"Stop doing whatever you're doing, I'm just loving it so much!" Hazel practically screamed at him.

"But I can't stop …" Cole answered shamefully. "Just can't. My sincere apologies though. Sorry. Oh wait then you want me to stop being myself? Man, that's got to be tough."

"I am actually ready to slap you any moment," Hazel said. "For real."

"Go ahead, a guy must take pain from a girl right?" Cole said.

She smacked him moderately.

"Ouch, that hurt," Cole spoke. "I know it did. Besides, I was going easy on you. I can make it hurt way more," Hazel howled. "Then do it. Keep slapping me, sure I can withstand it easy," Cole ordered.

"Not on me if you get injured or even die," Hazel said. "All you."

She smacked him several more times, withdrawing her hand every time to laugh for a couple of seconds.

Cole's cheeks were all red.

"You look like a swollen teddy bear…no wait red gummy bear, I almost feel sorry for you," Hazel said. "You compared me to something that can be chewed? How could you. And now I know you don't show mercy …so bet you won't even feel sorry a bit," Cole declared.

"I don't even know what to say," Hazel replied.

"That means I win. I'm victorious!" Cole shouted.

"Can't believe I just let you win, but if that's what makes you happy, I'll let you take it," Hazel yelled back in a coy tone.

"You're great, awesome, spectacular …" Cole said.

"Astronomical?" she pointed to the sky.

"Yea sure. That'd do," Cole agreed.

"I don't even know how to wrap things up now. I can't do anything else or move on," Hazel brought up. "No wait! There's a notebook and a pencil in the storage in front of your seat can you get it?"

"I'm on …" Cole got up and went to retrieve the objects.

He took them and came back, handing them to Hazel. She started scribbling. "What are writing down?" Cole asked intently. "Just something, you'll see," Hazel assured him.

At last, she picked up her pencil and turned the notebook over to Cole to take a look.

His eyes immediately saw that she had written a list. Hazel had numbered them, and looking closer, he realized what the words read: 1. Ocean, 2. Rooftop, 3. Church activity, 4. Cabin, 5. TBD (a lot more I'm going to add). "It's a way to keep track and organize fun stuff coming up for us. You know, I'm a girl who likes to have funnnn," Hazel puffed up her cheeks. "I forgot something, can I have them back for a sec?" Cole gave the notebook and the pencil to her. Peering over her shoulder, Cole watched her cross-out the first activity on the list…ocean. "We're doing that so it's pretty safe to say we're done with that," Hazel pointed out.

"I'm going to decorate it and try pictures of fun stuff on the sides," Hazel cheered. "I love it. Do so, I love making lists too," Cole nodded. "Ok, then that settles this," Hazel said.

"Nice, I think we should pack up now. I really don't want to," Cole told her. "Yeah, you're right," Hazel admitted. She waved "bye" to the ocean and hopped into the passenger seat since Cole was going to drive. Together, they left the area of brick paths and organized flower beds with enclosed fountains and ventured through the long road accompanied by fields of poppy and grass on either side.

They turned on the radio on the way back as the sky darkened and sang at the top of their lungs.

***

By the time they got back to the familiarity of the city, it was 8:30pm. "Hey how about we wrap up the day with some nightlife, like get a taste of that street-life downtown, because, to be honest, uptown is the boring part, and we live there so not to be mean, but it's true," Hazel suggested.

"Yeah, good idea, I'm up for that," Cole answered.

"Ok great! Then, let's go…" Hazel excitedly responded to him.

Hazel was a good driver and a speeder sometimes. She would guess when a police officer wasn't around and start swerving around the lanes like crazy to the point it would annoy fellow drivers. To Cole, she had always been like this, personality-wise, but in a graceful way.

Hazel zipped under the overpass, crossed through a tunnel that led into the heart of the city and ran pass on top of a bridge. Billboards hung on the sides of the roads next to separate communities. Cole had always travelled through this highway, so he was familiar with all the landmarks that aided with not getting lost or missing an exit.

Seattle was a bright city itself, and a rather populated one. Cole had long since lived there as a kid, and for a few generations back, his relatives had been there and never moved.

Hazel crossed the bridge and entered the streets of Seattle. Not surprisingly, there was a lot of traffic. Every block could take 10 minutes to get through, so Cole pulled out a map to find a shortcut.

"Why don't you use your phone?" Hazel asked him. "I don't have it on me...you know why," Cole lightly replied. "Oh yea, true, I didn't think about that, but I see now..." Hazel nodded.

They sped pass several blocks of restaurants and apartments. The city was like another world, unlike where they had gone previously. There were tons of people walking around and cars so close to one another that it seems as though everyone was about to crash. Also, there was constant honking everywhere.

"I never liked the city, but I like it for its brightness and liveliness," Hazel opinionated. "You serious? I've always loved the city," Cole countered. "What? How? Explain to me what this has to offer," Hazel made a show of displaying the world outside the car.

"Well, for one thing, it keeps you busy, and for another ..." Cole started. "What if you like to take it easy? I'm pretty sure you know I'm that type of person," Hazel explained. "Yes, mostly, but sometimes you're wild, and I *admire* that about you," Cole retorted.

"Oh! Stop it…" Hazel raised her eyebrows, sneaking a look at him.

So they made the turns: right, left, right, left, and so on.

"Ok, we're nearing, so I think we can find parking now…" Hazel brought up. "Got u," Cole answered.

Cole found a vacant space next to a meter and situated the car there. They both got out and Hazel was like, "So what street is this?" she glanced at the closest street sign. "Ok, this way," Hazel directed left.

It was chilly for a Seattle night, and so Hazel had taken out her jacket from the trunk of the car. "Hey, here's a spare one," she handed another jacket that was all black to Cole. "Fits your style, I believe."

"This was how you've always been …being the mindful gal who's always thinking of the people around her," Cole exclaimed. "Oh that was who I always was? Ok sure …tell me more about what you know about me from your "previous" …I don't know how to explain it …." Cole interjected, "You can say previous life? That'd work." "Ok. Previous life…sounds weird…but alright," Hazel agreed.

Cole started, "Well, we would go on some trips together and once, I'd forgotten my jacket and you even offered to give me your pink one." "Really? I was that nice?" Hazel asked sarcastically although she knew it. "Well you're certainly not a "not-nice" person so if you're not a "not-nice" then you're probably a nice person," Cole reasoned. "Sounds right," Hazel shrugged quickly. "Sounds like me."

"You saying that because you're trying to *show off?*" Cole joked. "No…no! I wouldn't!" she stared at him horrifically. "I'm not that bad. C'mon I thought you knew me well. Be serious for once!" Hazel retorted. "Hey who said a guy couldn't make fun of a girl?" Cole defended. "Uh…me, duh. Like sometimes I want to make you smarter but I don't think there is enough space in your brain …or maybe no space at all," Hazel decided.

"Possibly, not probable though," Cole agreed.

"Just to let you know …I try," Hazel coincided. "Wait a second. You just bragged again. I see. Bragging when you have the opportunity right? Like when my attention isn't here. Strategy," Cole pointed out.

Hazel slapped her face, clearly outraged.

"I am not talking to you for the rest of the time, mark my words," Hazel said. "Fine, then silent game it is …whoever loses has to go run around the block five times," Cole responded. "What kind of punishment is that? This is an example of not being intelligent …" Hazel laughed. "We'll soon see who shouldn't be talking … and who's more *intelligent,*" Cole muttered loudly. "I take that as a challenge?" Hazel questioned. "Of course," Cole confirmed.

They walked on, neither daring to talk. Hazel pointed for directions and kept her mouth shut.

Cole started doing sign language with his hands, and then Hazel couldn't help it. "What does that mean?" she inquired.

"You talked!" Cole cried.

Hazel, realizing her mistake, rolled her eyes. "It's okay, I'll run for you," Cole patted her.

Before she could say anything, he took off. In less than a minute, Cole had ran an entire lap and she watched him run the next four. At the end, Cole had returned and was panting like crazy. He hugged a sidewalk lamp for support and stayed put for a whole 30 seconds.

"Wow, I should be thankful I guess..." Hazel said timidly, looking up to the sky immediately after she'd said it and crossing her arms together so that her palms were clenching one another all the while straightening her posture. "You're welcome," Cole answered after he had caught his breath. "Thank you for talking."

"You didn't have to do it though. Did you do it because you ...oh now I see who's trying to show that they are the better person ..." Hazel broke into a smile. "Exactly," Cole confirmed. "Strategy?" Hazel asked.

"Of course girl," Cole corroborated.

"Never-mind, let's keep moving," Hazel turned around.

"Guys have got to have strategy to play the love game and chase and hopefully catch girls like you," Cole explained.

"This is common sense, I know this, it's completely *self-explanatory*," Hazel retorted. "Everyone knows this."

They strolled until they rounded a corner onto a narrow street of cobblestone. Strings of lanterns lit the street full of people and markets. Jazzy music was playing all around them. Big neon signs were beckoning customers inside bars.

"This is cool," Cole acknowledged.

They went around, looking at all the merchandise on sale and peering into restaurant windows, especially paying focus to the special dishes that were on the tables.

Hazel said, "I know there's a dinner with really good ice cream there, let's go get some …!"

"Oh, but I don't have money," Cole said.

"Don't worry, I'll pay for you, it's ok," Hazel beckoned. "Yeah but that's kinda embarrassing on my part," Cole answered. "See? Why do boys have to be like that? Can't the girl pay at least once?" she exaggerated. "You might as well, it's not like I can complain …" Cole smiled.

"Wait for me here, it should be real fast," Hazel told him. "Nah, I'll come in with you, it's all good," Cole said.

They ventured in and then both got a chocolate-vanilla ice cream, the one that was a swirl.

"I don't get it when people lick ice cream rather than eating it like I do right away," Cole told Hazel. "Like how are you doing it…why do people even lick ice cream I can't wrap my mind around that," he continued. Hazel seemed dumbfounded.

"I don't know. All I know is that I have never seen anyone *eat* ice cream before licking it," Hazel crossed her arms to appear convincing. "Wow, you're being salty to me ok I see how it is," Cole said like he knew what he was speaking about.

"Let's go to the park …I like it there," Hazel urged.

City parks were always the best. They were wide and spacious and had a lot of benches to sit on. Also, city parks were rather peaceful places in such a noisy environment.

Hazel and Cole headed to the park that was close to the nightlife streets, just across the road. Although much smaller than Central Park in New York City, this park might as well had the same elements as did its cousin. There were occasional streams and bike trails and lots of trees. All in all, it was a good hangout area for being social.

They arrived at a bench and sat down, taking in their surroundings.

"I like it here…a lot…very," Hazel said as she awed at the trees in sight and the towering buildings above her.

"I thought you hated the city?" Cole brought up.

"No, I change my mind, thanks to you," Hazel retorted.

"Ok, after all that was payback for making me run," Cole explained.

"Hey! That was *your* idea not mine!" Hazel protested.

"Since you're better than me …ok," Cole dismissed.

"You'll come to my party tomorrow right?" Hazel asked Cole. "Yours? Yes, of course, I've known you too well. The Hazel who knows me always knows I never miss a party of hers."

"7:30pm tomorrow don't be late …" Hazel eyed him warily.

"I'll be on time," Cole announced confidently. "Fine. Let's see if that's a promise you can keep," Hazel replied.

They headed back to Hazel's car and drove home.

When inside, Hazel stated, "Ok, that was a good day …I'll see you tomorrow in the morning? I'm making breakfast so you don't have to worry about that …" Cole answered, "That's a bet."

So Cole went upstairs and took a long, hot shower before changing into warmer clothes Hazel provided (she had a brother who had left clothes at her house).

Again, he thought about what had really happened to him as he lay on his bed, trying to piece it together. But still, Cole was clueless. Then, he was about to fall asleep when something in the room had caught his eye. It looked like a book.

He hurried over and took a long look at it. It was a photo album. Opening up, Cole saw pictures of Hazel with her family. She loved family, and her family was blessed to have her. She always went the extra mile for them whenever necessary.

But flipping through the pages, Cole couldn't find a picture that included him and her. This triggered his emotions. At last he couldn't stand at spotting only his absence. It seemed as if all those years of memories were ripped away, for Hazel had took countless pictures with him before, but the thought of them never happening was too overwhelming.

In anguish, he dropped down on his bed and put his hands on his face. Why did it have to be like this?

But the events of the day, probably maybe one of his best days ever, overcame him and sleep took ahold.

The next morning he awoke to a sudden jolt that was really nothing. He'd dreamed of the same incident and was surprised that the previous day wasn't all a dream. In fact, he'd woken up in Hazel's house, in the very same bedroom.

The sun shone clearly through the window and Cole turned to see the clock. It read: 11:30.

So late!

Cole hurriedly got out of bed and ran downstairs to see a note on the table. It was a strip of paper that read: "I know …you're tired and you couldn't eat my delicious eggs but whatever …gone out to buy lunch for both of us …" and then there was a smiley face with "love ya" next to it. Cole relaxed at this.

He waited for her to come home but then Archie licked him.

Archie was right there, and Cole had almost forgotten about Hazel's dog. Aside from Hazel not knowing who he is …the only other thing different was that she had a dog, which wasn't how it was.

When Hazel came home, Cole was sitting right there on the couch. "Hey boyfriend, good morning!" she cheered. Cole shuddered when she said "boyfriend" and he didn't know whether it was serious or not or maybe even neither.

Cole got up and helped her take the food to the dining table. He went to take the silverware because that was always his "task" every time they ate together at her house. "Wait why are you…" "Oh! It's just how we were …we gave each other a different job," Cole explained. "Oh I like that, ok let's do it that way," Hazel agreed. "So what's my job?" she asked. "You don't have one, I do it all," Cole told her. "For real? I can't imagine who I am. I must be terrible …where you came from," her eyes widened. "No, you fought me for it but I wanted to do it for you," Cole settled.

"And I see Archie is happy to see you!" she kneeled down and petted Archie and kissed him. "I really like your dog," Cole said. "Oh! Do you want to walk him later?" she inquired. "Yea…" "Plus it's *our* dog…" Hazel corrected, "There's a difference."

70

They ate and after that, Cole suggested, "We should watch TV, it's what we always did for fun you know." Hazel seemed to ponder this. "I guess so, let's do it."

They watched a show together and Hazel said she was cold halfway, so Cole took a blanket and put it over both of them to keep themselves warm. Hazel snuggled up to Cole and he did the same as they watched the episode ... it was heartwarming.

After, they went outside with Archie to the backyard. "So let me teach you... Archie likes it when you throw the ball straight into the air for him to catch. Remember, not far, but high up," Hazel informed him. "Ok, I'll try," Cole threw the ball up.

He threw the ball up, and sure enough Archie pounced up and caught the ball between his teeth, bringing it back to Cole. "He seems to like you a lot, that's a good sign," Hazel observed.

"Are you jealous?" Cole asked her. "Of what?" Hazel asked back.

"That he might like me more than you?" Cole questioned curiously. Hazel's expression clearly showed it but she denied it. "No, no way, I will never be jealous like this…not at all."

"Truth?" Cole asked once again. "Truth," Hazel replied, although it clearly was a lie.

"We should have secret codes or secret signs or something," Cole pointed out. "Then we're unique."

"Yeah, people would be like what are they doing while we're the only ones who will understand," Hazel acknowledged.

"So …got any ideas?" Cole prompted.

"Give me a minute, I'll think of one," Hazel lifted a finger. She was tapping her hip with her other hand, something she did when she herself was in deep thought.

Hazel's backyard was nice…it had a grand porch and a patio that was a decent size for the city. The neighborhood she lived in was also very good in terms of quality. For one thing, it was clean given the conditions in an urban setting and also it was welcoming.

"I need to prepare for tonight, so I'm going to go get supplies. Care to come? Or do you have other plans …" Hazel tapped his shoulder.

"I'm up, I don't think I would even know what to do by myself. You're like really the only person I actually am close to right now," Cole acknowledged. "Well then, let's roll," Hazel swung around on her foot towards the door.

Once again, they rode in the car together, Hazel taking the wheel. This time, however, they took Archie with them.

So Hazel started the engine while Archie hopped onto Cole's lap. "Aw he loves you!" Hazel observed.

They sped down the road and turned into a large avenue as Cole pet Archie who was panting and occasionally licking his arm. The wind rushed through their hair.

Hazel passed into a marketplace and parked the car. Together, they busted out, heading towards the mega-store. Hazel took Cole's hand, and he'd remembered how great it felt to hold her hand. Then they skipped through the sliding doors together, because it was like the old times. It seemed like it also dawned on Hazel as though she had a fragment of the memory from before although it was obvious that couldn't be true. She was from this reality not the one Cole was from. Anyway, a shopping spree was a perfect hangout for them, and they were excited.

The store mostly had groceries but also other things too. "Ok, you know I like making lists …so since I forgot to bring paper, I'll make a mental note …first we need cups and plates and all that," Hazel told him. "By the way, do you want to split up or …" she started. "I think it would be more fun if we did it together …just like the old times," Cole said even though he knew she had no experience of the past with him. However, given her unique personality, she played along with it.

Grocery stores were always POIs for them. While everyone was off to the movies or the mall, they would go to grocery stores. They specifically liked the different aisles, because imagine all the things you could do with them. Just the idea of different items being grouped together in sections has evolved to games they would play.

"There's a game we used to play …and that's how I push you on the cart while you're standing on the foothold below and then wherever you land, we'll buy the stuff there. But first, you have to pick a number without looking ..." Cole shielded her eyes with his palm.

"I choose ...5!" Hazel declared.

They headed to aisle five, which turned out to be the aisle for cereal boxes and things of that sort.

Cole put Archie in the shopping cart but then Hazel cried, "No! He doesn't like that ..."

"He's a very engaging dog who likes to be part of the action ...sorry for scaring you though," Hazel explained.

"No you're good ...I guess I don't really know him THAT well," Cole admitted. "But I'll get to know him no worries."

"I love your positive attitude, it makes me feel hopeful too," Hazel nudged him in the side.

"You just nudged me in the side," Cole laughed. "Now I'm going to be negative so you'll be negative."

"UH, that's actually not how it works, dude. Your positive attitude only makes me feel more hopeful but you being negative still makes me feel hopeful because, as you know,

I'm one hopeful gal," Hazel corrected him. "I do believe that from the bottom of my heart," Cole made a show of bowing down. "Thanks," Hazel cheeked, suppressing a smile.

Hazel stood on the cart and Cole got ready for a big push. "You ready?" he asked.

"Always," she answered mischievously.

Cole took a few steps back, took several large steps forward, and then flung the cart down the aisle.

Archie ran after the cart, trying to be a part of the action.

Meanwhile, Hazel was yelping in fear, her eyes widened. Cole had indeed given a hard push.

At least there wasn't anyone in the role, which was a relief. She would have probably crossed the other end of the aisle if it weren't for the cereal box that lay on the ground. The left front wheel hit the box and the shopping cart skidded to a stop.

Hazel bent over there, catching her breath while Cole jogged to her. "Too fast? C'mon I thought you could take that."

"Hey! It's my first time! Don't judge me …" Hazel snapped with intimidation.

"I guess that's a valid reason … I'll let you go on this one, but this one only don't get me wrong," Cole warned.

"Let's see what we have here."

It was a whole section full of different types of oatmeal. "You think your guests would like oatmeal?" Cole asked her. "I mean I wouldn't have problem with this."

Hazel rolled her eyes. "Let's take it. It's a rule right? You have to take something when you stop at that section?"

"That's true," Cole acknowledged.

"Well then, it's not like I have any options, so I say we get it," Hazel concluded.

Cole grabbed several boxes of oatmeal and on they went.

"Other than food, we need drinks, and a loud speaker. I have everything else," Hazel informed.

So it was a mission. Cole launched the cart with Hazel on it every few feet because they thought it would go faster although it was obvious it wasn't making their "journey" quicker.

There was a lot of "let's get this" or "let's get that" from both of them so they ended with a filled-up cart with items from basically every section in the store. It was like they bought the entire place.

Self-checkout was always the best part.

"I love the scanning …it's so satisfying!" Hazel exclaimed. "Me too," Cole replied.

"I call scanning!" Hazel cried. "And you sir …take packing."

"Wow really? Giving me the *worser* job?" Cole protested.

"Yes, cuz you're the worser person, and the worser person deserves a worser job, and I'm superior," Hazel explained.

"That's just great," Cole responded.

So Hazel started scanning and handing them to Cole to bag them and put them in the shopping cart. Archie was jumping onto his hind legs to try to take a look into every grocery bag. "Hey Archie, I'll let you see later, but please let us finish first," Hazel pet him.

Archie was an obedient dog so he released his grip on the scan counter and dropped to the ground, resuming his panting.

"He really listens to you," Cole observed.

"Yes, that is correct," Hazel answered.

"I wish you listened to me," Hazel muttered softly but apparent enough for Cole to hear.

"I do!" he cried.

"Oh no you don't, unlike him," she pointed to Archie who was glaring beadily at them with his kind eyes.

"Well, I see how it is," Cole concluded.

"C'mon, stop talking and help me put these bags into the cart. Look at how many items are sitting right there for you that haven't been scanned. I can multitask somehow and you cannot?" Hazel pushed him lightheartedly. "You will never survive in a factory."

"Not unless I get somebody who doesn't work as fast and as well as you …then yes," Cole retorted.

"I know you won't like that. You'd prefer me," Hazel stopped for a moment.

Cole contemplated this.

"I think you're right. I really won't like that. Yes. I see now."

Hazel looked away, smiling. She was almost done scanning all the items and Cole was working at a faster rate than before to prove that he could come-back.

"Don't try impressing me ... it will never ever work ... I don't get swayed easily," Hazel nudged him in the chest. "Well ... there's good news for me ... cuz I don't have to," Cole pointed out. "What do you mean?" she asked back. "You know what I mean," Cole winked. "Oh like you don't have to impress me because you've already got me? That's false," she said. "No, its big facts," Cole stated.

"Big facts?" Hazel howled. "Ha-ha, big facts. I don't know, you're one heck of a guy."

"Is that a compliment? Thank you," Cole replied.

"No, in fact, it's the opposite of one. So you should be saying no thank you to me," Hazel explained readily. "Next time listen first."

"Wow you got me there … smart. Now I'm done," Cole answered.

"Not done cuz I'm giving you mercy," Hazel pursed her lips. "Mercy? You're so nice to give me mercy? I'm not going to take it though," Cole responded.

"But I'll make you take it so you have no choice … sorry," and she bent her head down and pressed her lips together to act like she truly meant what she was saying.

"The way you do that is cute … like I gotta be honest with ya," Cole phrased. "Why… is that a compliment? Thank you!" Hazel cheered and smiled as if she was a cartoon character.

"I can't counter that … you're good at it. Like taking what I did to you and using it against me but in an easy, casual, slick way," Cole retorted. "Yeah, yeah," Hazel nodded.

"I wish I could be you … or be part of your gang … but I hate you so I can't," Cole hackled. "Oh you really mean that?" Hazel asked. "I can't answer that so I'll keep that *confidential, fyi,*" Cole explained. "Yeah cuz you legit don't have anything to say," Hazel bounced back.

"Oh well, it is how it is," Cole sighed and let loose a breath of air.

"I'm a wild but also *ideal* girl so bear with me. Being with me takes a toll to let you know. Brace yourself," Hazel warned.

"That's how you always were," Cole countered. "I am well aware and am well trained and prepared. Also, I know the price this is gonna take."

"Woah! So confident! Are you only saying that so you would appear like a man although …" Hazel started. "No, no, it's from my heart," Cole answered.

"I'm trusting you on this one. Wait until you're tested," Hazel shook him. "There are tests? You never told me that!" Cole protested. "Yes, and they will be tough, like actually tough," Hazel raised her eyebrows.

"Nothing is too hard for me when it comes to you …" Cole said, and Hazel couldn't suppress her giggle. She just looked away at the aisle plates, smiling and at a loss for words. It was the best thing a guy had ever said to her and it was every girl's dream.

Cole didn't know how to react. He just delivered probably one of the best lines ever, and it had slipped out of him like liquid. They stood there, both uncomfortable for what felt like centuries, sometimes locking eyes and sometimes looking away at other things.

Finally, Cole said, "Hey! I almost forgot! The packing's all done. Let's head home!" and before he could turn away, Hazel felt the palm of his right hand with two fingers and then Cole took initiative and clasped his hand over hers.

As they strode out together, Hazel spoke softly, "I really liked what you said." She looked up to him. Cole smiled back.

Hazel opened the trunk and they put the bags in.

Right when they got into the car, Hazel's head leaned onto Cole's shoulder for several minutes and they sat in silence while they watched the world unfold in front of them through the car window.

Not before long, Cole realized Hazel had fallen asleep on his shoulder and so he gently got out of the car, moved Hazel to the driver's sleep (she was a very tight sleeper so she usually never woke up), took her keys, and then started driving.

From there, they headed home through the large avenues of the suburbs of Seattle, pass restaurants and other marketplaces, bars and clubs, and then finally houses.

Cole pulled through the welcome sign that was engraved in the stone and then made a few turns to get back to Hazel's house.

He parked her car up front next to the sidewalk and then went to pick her up from the other side. Cole took one hand to lift the area behind her chest and another hand to hold steady the back of her knees. Doing this, he marched up to the front door, opened it, and went in. Cole immediately walked up the stairs to her bedroom and set her on the bed. He tugged several blankets onto Hazel to keep her warm and then slipped a pillow under her head. She was sound asleep, and maybe even more to the adjustments Cole had made.

Then something came to Cole's mind.

It has been over 24 hrs since he had landed in something that seemed like an alternate reality from the previous one he knew about. He was going to investigate what really happened. Cole was curious, although he was having second thoughts on trying to go back cuz right now, it just seemed so right to stay.

Hazel and he were getting along, so what was the need to go back? But then he thought of Hazel in the previous reality or dimension and if they were the same person. Characteristically, they no doubt were, but how come she didn't know him here and when did Hazel get the dog that was lapping at his ankles right now?

Curiosity won the best of him. He was going to go back to where he thought he'd landed to investigate and understand what truly occurred regardless if he wanted to stay or not.

Cole looked back at Hazel who was soundly asleep. She was so peaceful. He went over and sat on the couch next to the bed, watching her in her sleep, tracing out all the beautiful features of her. How calm she was, like the sway of a gentle breeze.

Exhale, inhale, exhale, inhale.

Cole found a pen and a notebook full of paper and then ripped one of them out. He wrote a note saying that he "went somewhere" so she need not have to worry about him. Cole also wrote that he would try to make it back to the rooftop party she was hosting (he had seen her texting like thousands of people before) tonight and that he already had the address and time. Cole then pet Archie and said bye to him. "I'll come back bro," he assured Archie.

And with that, Cole strolled out of the room, down the stairs, and out of the house. He walked a few miles to a nearby bus station and waited for the correct one to come.

Finally, a bus with "Olympic National Park" on it arrived and he boarded the vehicle, remembering to pay the fare through coins he had borrowed from Hazel's coin jar.

It was time to unravel the confounding mystery.

It took about 2hrs to get there but it was still 3:30pm and the party wasn't supposed to start until a couple hours later so he was good. He didn't want to let her down by not going. It wasn't cool because she would never do the same to him.

The bus dropped all the tourists off at the welcome center and sped off, leaving all of them alone. It suddenly dawned on Cole that he had forgotten which meadow he had landed in.

But luckily, he had remembered the surrounding features of the area. There were tall trees, some coniferous, and the meadow had tall, yellow grass that were so straight they were extremely vulnerable to the direction the wind blew them. It was also on top of a high hill because he recalled that somewhere off of the meadow, there was a great overlook that displayed the entire city across the bay.

People were walking around everywhere, many of them nature lovers and adults obsessed with national parks. Cole deducted that the place should be east of the park, probably close to the edge, given that it had a great view of the city.

And he was going to have to do it by foot.

So Cole made it a goal to boost his motivation and started trudging around. He brushed through the park at a surprising speed and overcame many fields that looked almost identical to what he remembered. However, he knew they were the wrong ones after looking closer and every time this was the circumstance, he would assure himself that he should keep looking because he will find the right one. Giving up didn't even cross his mind. Curiosity fueled his soul.

Cole made his way east and stayed close to the shoreline next to the ocean because they were the vantage points. He was becoming to feel anxious because he didn't have a watch on him or anything that would tell him time, and the sky was dimming.

He couldn't miss the party, plus he had to find the place or else he wouldn't be satisfied.

Cole was sweating by now, the walk had gotten a toll on him. He saw various people walk by him to the welcome center to go home and he really wanted to turn around and head back. But he couldn't give up or it would've been a wasted opportunity. But he was tired, so tired. If it hadn't been a miracle, he spotted the meadow up ahead to his right. There it was, lying right in front of him.

"Oh!" Cole yelped in surprise.

He struggled and jogged over, breathing heavily from exhaustion. The lactic acid had started kicking in.

There he was again. Cole saw the great overlook a little away from the small meadow.

It was the same place, he knew it. Cole tried to locate the exact space he had landed so he started looking up at the trees and adjusting his angle of seeing them to find the spot.

And then his foot stepped onto something and it give a different sound, one you wouldn't expect from a meadow.

He picked up his foot and moved it away, glancing down.

It was a photograph, the ones that had a white border around them that was only several centimeters, and he recognized it was Hazel. He blinked and looked one more time... it was her.

He remembered it. Only his arm was seen in the photo cuz he was accidentally cut out but really the photo was concentrated on Hazel, smiling and peering at the camera.

They were at a roller skating rink and he recalled her falling multiple times and himself having to hold her hand so she would stop. Cole personally thought ice skating was harder, but it turned out roller skating was a tougher one for Hazel because she excelled at ice skating like a pro while Cole was falling everywhere on the ice.

She was wearing a light purple t-shirt and jeans, and her smile was flashing.

So why was there a picture of her here? How did it get here?

Everything just got a whole lot more confusing. Cole recognized this was the spot, exactly where he landed. There were no other clues around, just the photograph. He knew the sky was darkening so he pocketed the picture and ran back towards the welcome center. It took a while to get back but he never stopped to take a break.

Cole got onto a bus that took him straight to the address.

He asked the bus driver, "What time is it?" and the bust driver replied, "6:00 sir." Cole started to panic because the party was supposed to start at 7:30pm but he realized he could still make it but be late for 30 minutes and get there by 8 o'clock.

Thankfully, traffic wasn't that congested, and the bus had gotten to the station nearest the address in midtown Seattle by 7:45 pm. Cole payed, hopped off, and then searched for the address.

He found a medium-height building that was maybe 20 stories high nestled between several skyscrapers.

Hazel had said that the party was on the 15th floor but she never said which room or apartment or condo or whatever.

So Cole went through one of the entrances where you push the door in a circle to get to the other side and then approached the receptionist at the counter.

"Yes? What are you here for?" the receptionist asked.

"Oh, I'm just here for a friend by the name of Hazel Francesca?"

"Ok, just take those elevators and it'll take you right there."

"May I ask which room?" Cole inquired.

"Yes, it's not a room, it's a large condo with a grand balcony. But yes, suite 1568," the receptionist answered.

Cole went to the elevator and pressed the "up" button. He entered it and then pressed the 15 button.

Cole didn't know what to expect. Hazel had once thrown a house party and it was actually pretty crazy. All her friends from high school had come but she mostly stuck with Cole. It was weird. Although she had a lot of friends, Hazel preferred to stay with Cole. She just made it an occasion for everyone to have fun with each other while she sat back. Even though Hazel did chat with everyone she knew, she liked the company of Cole more than all of her buddies. Ding! The doors slid open to reveal a large open-concept living and dining room combo with a large bar that had a glass island and then a gigantic balcony.

But it was Hazel that freaked him out the most. She was standing there, arms-crossed, with a straight expression, right in front of the elevator. Cole jumped.

"Where'd ya go? What took you so long?"

Cole saw that the whole room was full of people their age, a couple he recognized.

He motioned her to the side, next to the kitchen sink.

"You got something to say?" Hazel was pretty angry it seemed, but since there were so many people, she kept it in a moderate tone. "You know, I was worried for you."

"Listen, I had to do something, sorry for coming in late," Cole explained thoroughly.

"That's it? That's how specific you can get? You had to do something," Hazel mimicked.

Cole was about to say something before Hazel shrugged and said, "I'll just forget about it, now have a good time, I'll show you around."

Hazel brought Cole around to introduce him to others. "So this is Jackie, she's like one of my besties," Hazel showed him. "Hey!" Jackie waved to Cole. "Hey," Cole replied.

Hazel brought him to a few other people. All in all, there were probably 30 people in that massive condo. There was one large room combining the living room and kitchen and also separate medium-sized rooms off the large room. But the game-winner and deal-breaker was the glass balcony hanging off of the massive room.

"This is Sophia, she's super chill," she introduced. "Hey!" Cole said. "Nice meeting ya." Sophia replied, "You too." "He's a new friend," Hazel told Sophia.

Cole knew both of these people but they obviously didn't know him.

"Ok, so I'm going to go to the balcony to chit-chat with some acquaintances so suit yourself," Hazel told him. "Come join me when you feel like it …"

They departed ways and Cole went over to the bar to grab a drink. He wasn't feeling alcohol (the bottles they had bought that day) so he went with orange soda instead. Cole poured himself a glass of orange soda and put some ice cubes into it.

He watched the bubbles sizzle on top for several seconds until they died off and it became plain.

Cole stepped onto the balcony and there was pop music being played. The balcony was magnificent. There were lights across the walls and banisters as well as potted plants to create an outdoors look. There were metal round tables with chairs that had umbrellas on top of them. The balcony was glass but the sides of the building had wood-plank tiles. There was also brick and some stone. Also, as a bonus, there were beach-style reclining chairs that were fit for an urban setting. Furthermore, there was a fish tank in the middle.

Something Hazel would do ... rent a space to throw a random party for only one night.

There were strings of lights on top of the balcony stretching from one side to the other to illuminate the place. It gave a very bright vibe and probably contributed to the mood of the guests.

But the view was stunning. There was a 180 degree view of the city. Colorful skyscrapers were seen from high above in every angle. You could see the buildings 10 miles away and across the bay to Olympic National Park. Looking down, all the cars looked like ants crawling around their paths, the roads.

Cole stood gaping at the view, unable to take his eyes off of it.

"I see you, you like it don't you?" Hazel asked, suddenly next to him.

"Yeah, it's quite splendid," Cole replied.

"I choose a great place?" Hazel questioned.

"Oh yeah," Cole answered, his eyes still attached to the skyline.

"Inside is even better …through the glass," Hazel informed him.

"No, this is already really nice," Cole replied.

"Waterfront would've been better, or maybe even a yacht, I should've done that you know …that'd be fun," Hazel explained.

"No, I like this," Cole responded.

"Really?"

"Really."

"OH! Where's Archie?" Cole suddenly realized. "Right behind you," Hazel pointed out.

And before Cole could register this, Archie leap onto his shoulders.

This startled him. "Man, this is one high jumper."

"What are we going to do?" Cole asked. "Well, I usually like to supply the material and have everyone do what they'd like. There's a machine that gives off steam and bubbles …don't know why I bought that. I also have some water balloons and water guns for no reason but I doubt anyone would use those. We could play tag I mean or some board games. I've also got some beach balls lying around and a game of cup pong going on over there, but mainly I like to socialize that's it as host," Hazel rumbled. "Wow how long have you been planning this? Like when did you get the idea? You set it all up today right?" Cole questioned.

"C'mon I'm not slow like you ...I'm fast, speedy," Hazel told him.

"Wow thanks," Cole rolled his own eyes.

"Oh wait, there's also food, if you're hungry by any chance," Hazel brought up.

Cole knew he was hungry from all the walking.

"Also, you smell kinda bad too ...did you just go the gym or something?" she asked.

"I did get some exercise but no," Cole replied.

So Cole went to get some food and then filled his empty stomach. It was a barbeque with many grilled things but also other cooked dishes that Hazel said she had ordered. There was also salad, desserts, and it was like a buffet with everything.

Cole kept going for more and more rounds until at last he was satisfied.

The others just casually ate whenever they felt like it unlike him and resumed their conversations. He got enormous plates of food every time and couldn't resist the urge of not savoring.

Everyone else enjoyed their time by eating slowly to prolong the time they could desire for the deliciousness of the food. Cole dove right in and ate to the point he couldn't eat no more. Just looking at the food made him sick to think of it.

Cole got that painful feeling in the back when you stuff too much down your throat at once and then it's like your whole body is cramping up. No one seemed to notice this.

Alas, he was just sitting by the corner of the massive balcony, not really doing anything or thinking. He was just there, in the moment. There were always those few stages in your life where you'd just be in the moment and stare-off into space.

Hazel walked over and sat across from him.

"How'd you like it?" she asked.

"Well, it could be more exciting. Remember that one I planned at some random ballroom in town? Now *that* was lit," Cole answered.

"Oh so you're saying that this isn't fun here??" Hazel questioned.

"Sort of, but not really. I said it in an indirect way," Cole replied. "Rooftop parties are nice … I think."

"Nice? Just nice? C'mon let's go downstairs. I booked another room because I don't know … they said someone else wanted this place in like half an hour … so we have to move. And I didn't want this to be short … so let's go now," Hazel urged him.

"Wait, before we go … I added so much more to our list," Hazel told him. "Take a quick glance, I've got plans for you and me."

Hazel took out the notebook and Cole realized that number three was crossed out: the church activity. "Oh yea, don't worry about that … it was cancelled a few hours ago … when you were a missing person," Hazel explained. "They said there would be some weather condition going on … like a lot of rain."

"That's sad," Cole said, but he continued to look through the list.

It read: 1. Ocean (crossed out)

2. Rooftop (semi-crossed out)

3. Church Activity (crossed out)

4. Cabin / Camp / waterSports / Lake Retreat / Mountains / shooting stars and northern lights

5. Concert

6. Laser Tag

7. Sports Game

8. Fruit Picking / Farm

9. Go Kart, Amusement Park, Bumper Cars

10. Eat-outs in Between 1-9

11. Cruising

12. Playground

13. National Park / the Hills / sunrise & sundown

"I don't get it. How will we finish all of this?" Cole asked her. "I'm just tryna have a good time, you know. If I never knew you, I would not make this list. Doing it alone is not the beauty of it. Doing it with someone else is the best part ..." Hazel responded.

"Wait what is playground ...like I don't understand," Cole inquired once more. "I've always sneaked into the playground at night to speak with friends and it'd always been my childhood place," Hazel exclaimed.

"So now I want to do it with you …" Hazel continued. Cole gently nodded. "Ok."

Cole recalled Hazel always being the one who liked to be outside at night, preferably the playground. Once, in 5th grade, she'd left her house out of her window at 2am and went to the playground. Hazel had made Cole promise he would be there, and so, being the person who wouldn't ever let her down, he showed up.

They would talk about life together on the swings and hide in various places of the playground. He knew about her inner feelings and she knew his in comparison. Just sitting there under the starlight some nights brought tranquility between them. It was something powerful.

"Man, we've been talking for some time …let's head downstairs, everyone's already making their way," Hazel snapped unsteadily. Cole proceeded towards the elevator.

"This is 3rd floor we're going to," Hazel told him. And so they entered, where Cole pushed the 3 button and down they went.

When the doors opened, it revealed a significantly smaller room where everyone had to cram together in a pack. "I couldn't find anything larger so this is the best," Hazel shrugged.

There was, however, a balcony that was smaller than the previous one. Cole headed onto it.

He went to the railing and then leaned on it. It felt unstable, and before he could straighten up, the railing gave way. The last thing he knew was that he just lost his balance and gravity was pushing him down through open space towards the hard ground.

"Cole!" Hazel cried, and she dove down after him. Cole didn't have time to process anything before he'd hit something that was somehow not the ground. Judging from smell, it was the dumpster probably, and the trash bags may have just saved his life.

Hazel crashed onto him from above, and they both winced.

Cole wanted to say something, but before he could, they were suddenly drawn to each other.

Hazel gazed into his eyes with a longing expression as Cole peered back exactly the same.

Hazel put her arms around Cole's neck and then their heads got closer. They placed their lips together and kissed. Her lips were soft and moist, hot and breathy, not trying to win a battle but seeking union and closeness and the sharing of a singular breath. It was one sensation, a timeless and passionate moment. Her lips brushed his, softly, delicately, like butterfly wings, just long enough that he could inhale her breath, feel the warmth of her skin. Hazel tasted him as he tasted her, and they felt their bond grow into something. Once, they were two, now they were one. It was a merging like no other. The gap was closed. It was complete. The circle was once half-filled, but now it was all filled.

Hazel broke away, smiling, and Cole smiled back. They kissed again, turning them into taunting pecks. It didn't matter that it smelled so bad there. It didn't matter that it had started pouring. It didn't matter that there were stains all across their clothes. It didn't matter that everybody above was watching them. What mattered was the other person, and they wanted more of each other.

They were so dirty, in a dumpster together, but yet, they wanted to have each other. They couldn't take enough, it was like their lives depended on this moment. It was desperate gulps of air as if they were drowning.

Hazel moved her lips over Cole's and he responded by kissing her neck in some spots as she closed her eyes. They rolled over and both dropped onto the hard tar of a damp road into a puddle. It was a small road, one no cars were allowed on.

Although they were wet, it was okay. Hazel wanted more of Cole, and he wanted more of her. It was blissful. They lay there, occasionally kissing and sometimes staring at each other with a smile. Her hair was dirty, his pants were soaked, but they loved each other the same. It was the spirit that roused in them.

"I love you," Hazel spelled out.

"I love you too," Cole spoke softly.

"I don't know what I would do without you," Hazel said back slowly.

"Me neither," Cole agreed.

"It's so great having you around ...like wherever I go," Hazel exclaimed. "Just you being here ...it brightens me," she continued. Cole laughed, "Well you're welcome. No problem. I love it when you talk, I love it when you're there, I love it when you are Hazel."

"I love it when you're Cole," Hazel answered.

She caressed his cheek and drew shapes on his skin. "That's ticklish, stop...!" Cole fought back an urge to break-away. "Can't stop me now ...I'm going to do whatever," Hazel bounced back.

"From now on, let's spend every day of our lives together," Hazel suggested. "Let's be together forever."

"I really like you," Cole confessed. "I'm going to have to say yes."

Hazel smiled and hugged him. Cole was happy. She was happy.

It was the following Monday morning in Hazel's house, and Cole had gotten accustomed to her ways. She was very flexible in her lifestyle, and Cole knew this because he'd known her much of his own life. The clicked so well that it seemed like they were never going to argue. Although they had minor disagreements, there was always a way they compromised. It was the beauty of their relationship.

But still, Cole thought of the day he'd mysteriously appeared in what seemed like a parallel reality. He wanted so badly to know how this happened, and so he realized he needed to take a solo retreat without Hazel. But he couldn't just leave her, because last time he'd left several hours, and Hazel was worried to death for him.

But he had to do it, because curiosity always got the best of him.

So he huffed up his courage, and Cole found Hazel in her room. "Hey, I have something to tell you."

Hazel lay on her stomach on her bed and shot up a glance. "What?"

Cole repeated, "Yes, I have something to talk to you about."

"You look nervous. You know you can tell me anything …it's alright," Hazel assured him. "Yeah, but this might be different," Cole responded a tad too abruptly.

"Go ahead, I'm ready," Hazel urged him.

"Listen, I think I need to get away for a bit, I have stuff to think about," Cole said, but he didn't want to reveal that he wanted to take time off by himself to try to piece-together everything in his mind. April shrugged, "Ok then let's pack our bags and go …"

"No! This is going to sound bad. I don't want to you to come with me," Cole cried and he immediately regretted how that came out. Although Hazel was a strong girl, she had feelings too, and it was apparent. She looked away towards the floor and Cole knew he had done something really wrong.

"Hey, um…" Cole started, but April put her hand up.

"I get it, I get it, you don't want me there …go," April stuttered with hurt in both her eyes and her voice, not making eye-contact with Cole. "That's not the worst part...I thought you'd tell me everything, but there's something you're hiding. Is it that you're confused about everything around you right now and where you're *from?*" She said this with an emphasis on the last word.

Tears started to build up in her eyes. He'd really cracked her, and he felt bad. "Hazel, I can explain..." Cole attempted, and he also started getting teary and a few drops left his eyelids.

"No, do whatever, it's okay, I'll be waiting for you." Cole made an executive decision and turned around, not looking back. He walked down the stairs, suddenly weary, and out the front door. Cole walked to the nearest metro station and then boarded one. He didn't know where he should be going but he went on whichever one came first and stayed on board until the last stop. The subway was very empty, and he was one of the only in the cart. The world flashed by him, and he looked straight forward, oblivious to everything.

Without Hazel, he felt a pang of loneliness, but he knew he would go back one day after he unlocked the truth to the mystery.

"Hang on, Hazel, I will come back," he muttered to himself quietly. "Just give me some time, and I will come back for you."

Cole told himself that it wasn't the end, but rather merely the beginning of it all.

PART TWO

Several months have passed, and Cole was on his own. He originally started with a few hundred dollars in his pocket but had gotten a job as a waiter in a restaurant in Portland, Oregon. From Seattle, Cole went south to Portland and established a living there. He was renting a one-room apartment that wasn't so appealing to any average person …but at least it was cheap, and in his free time, he would go out to the park and sit on the bench to think. Thinking was something he did a lot; it was a daily routine. Thoughts boggled his mind all the time. Mainly, he'd become one of the people that observed the world and didn't too much themselves. Cole wanted to get to know the fundamentals of everything …of nature, of people, of communities. It was habitual.

There was one thing he couldn't get rid of. He missed Hazel. He missed her so so much. But his time wasn't up yet, and Cole could sense it. Just a little longer, please patient, he would mutter into the air, hoping that somewhere across space and time, Hazel would get it. Every day, when he had that urge to go back and find her, he would say this to himself. It was both a method and distraction.

Besides, he didn't want to admit it, but he was afraid of how different things may seem if he went back now. Cole kept shunning this thought out, but it still bothered him. Time was the cause of difference. Over time, things change and become different, sometimes radically, sometimes only a tad. But nevertheless, there was always change.

How would she react to him re-appearing after all this time?

That was the main concern of his.

Anyway, he took it easy these days. Most days were uneventful. He barely had any friends, and there wasn't any excitement in his life. But Cole was glad that he'd found a job and a place to stay and seemingly have things figured out to live a stable life. Cole thought of Hazel sometimes to keep himself motivated. Just thinking of her kept him going. He thought of the couple days they shared together before he left, and they were probably the best days of his life. Cole missed all the fun and her company. She was a true friend and companion, and he'd turned it down and left her by herself. It was a mean thing, but Cole had to do it. He had to take time off of her. It was painful, but necessary.

How was she doing right now? Cole didn't know.

Some days he would not be able to fall asleep thinking of her and the possibilities she'd be living in right now. He would look out the window for hours and try to feel how she was feeling. Cole wanted to share emotions with Hazel, and he hoped she wanted too. And sometimes, Cole would even question if she felt the same for him.

Or maybe she forgot all about me already, he thought.

But no way. Hazel kept promises. She said they would be with each other forever until the end of time, and her words came back to him occasionally. Stuff she said was powerful, and it made Cole tremble uncomfortably but peacefully. Her words were reassuring, and he was hoping they would be true.

Cole sat in a café, sipping on iced coffee. It was around 2pm in Portland, and the city did what other cities did … big groups of people walking around, cars honking each other, planes flying overhead, everyone attending to their duties. This was the world.

He'd taken a day off from his job to really do nothing. Somedays, working didn't seem great at all, so he would call his manager and he would let him go. But other days, work allowed him a temporary escape from his thoughts, and it worked magnificently.

Cole sighed. He was bored. Was life about activities and fun? What was the purpose of life?

Cole got up and strode out of the café. He crossed a street and entered the bookstore there. Inside, he went over to the psychology section and picked up a random book to read. Reading had been a favorite pastime of his since he didn't really have any goals. Cole was quite satisfied and content with the basics of life, but it seemed like there was still something missing.

Hours passed when he read. If the book was fascinating enough, an entire morning plus afternoon could do until they forced him out because the store was closing. Most people bought the books to bring home to read, but not him. Cole read them all there, and he'd gotten through several aisles of them.

Cole was reading something about lizards, and it always intrigued him how lizards thought of life. They always seemed so joyful that they could scurry around trees and provide the food they needed. He watched the squirrels outside run up and down the trees. They would also pick up food on the ground and start chipping away. Cole thought of these creatures, and he wondered if humans were similar to their behavior. Some days, he could relate to their actions.

Hazel.

Hazel wasn't there with him. He saw all the squirrels with their companions. One would leap out and grab a fry on the ground and before you knew it, another came out just behind it. All the animals came in two, and so as humans.

In addition to going to the bookstore, Cole would go the gym, to work, stay at home, the park, or the harbor and bay. The waterfront was on the edge of the city, and it was ideal location to head to if you wanted to leave city life for a few hours. Just watching the waves roll back and forth reminded him of the day on the beach when everything started. Why did he have to go surfing?

But again, what occurred was something that couldn't be explained.

Then right there, something hit him.

Cole remembered the picture he'd found where he'd appeared in this parallel dimension. He never washed the pants and he looked down, seeing that he was wearing the same joggers. Then, with a hand, he reached into a pocket and pulled out the photograph of Hazel at the roller skating rink with him. However, it never occurred to him that he had never turned it around. On the back, at the bottom left corner, was his own signature. But Cole knew for certain he never signed his name on the back of this picture before, so this was strange. How'd it get there? There was no way someone forged it, because it wasn't too perfect but it also wasn't apparent that someone had tried to sign the name. Someway, he'd written his signature there and it stuck without him ever knowing. Cole thought of the wave, and in it he'd seen images of his life flash inside the water. Could it have been true that the picture had flown out of the water and landed with him in the meadow?

That was clearly impossible, but again, everything around him was clearly impossible. Cole wanted to cry, and run to a safe zone. But there was not safe zone, and no one knew about this except him. He was alone, the only one with the knowledge of what happened. Somewhere unreachable, probably the *real* Hazel he knew his whole life was trying to find him. That meant he was a lost soul, a lost boy.

Patience was beginning to run out on him, so he couldn't be telling Hazel to wait any longer if he couldn't handle it himself. It was so weird and such a horrible thing …getting pulled away from everyone and everything you ever knew and having it all replaced with basically the same thing except that the person who've always liked didn't know you anymore and then there was no explanation for the event.

Cole had to remain strong, for it was all he could do.

He heard music, and it came from one of those people who played on the streets. It was a man in his 50s strumming a guitar, and he was singing alongside his playing. People were dropping money into his case as they walked by and Cole eagerly headed towards him, drawn to the beautiful singing of his voice.

The man winked at him and smiled for a split-second as a greeting. Cole asked him, "Can I try? I think I need some music in my life right now." The guy said, "I see you need it, you look like you're having a rough day," and he handed over the guitar along with the strap.

Cole took the guitar and put the strap over him. Then, he casually sat on a flat rock and started strumming chords he recalled from other songs. And with that, he sang with all his spirit.

People from all directions came to him and joined him, creating a tight circle. They were sharing in the moment. It was powerful. The assembly of so many, all sharing a distinct feeling. Even the man was enjoying it. Not everyone knew the lyrics, but it didn't matter.

At the conclusion of the song, people started leaving, and Cole handed the guitar back to the man who applauded him. "No, it's because of you …you helped me back up," Cole pointed out when the guy started talking about how good he was. "Thank you instead."

"You inspired me to continue …thank you," Cole told the man, and the man nodded and gave a farewell salute. Cole saluted back and turned around, where they parted ways.

He didn't know when he would finally understand everything, but he was ready to start a new life.

Today was the day he'd gotten a new license so he could drive. Knowing that it was too pricey to purchase a new car, Cole rented a cheap sedan so he wouldn't have to always take the bus or metro. The sedan wasn't the best, but at least it brought him places.

It was already mid-autumn, and the leaves started to turn brown, yellow, and red. The temperature dropped and more wind came. Cole bought a down jacket to keep himself warm because he knew sooner or later, it would be freezing.

Cole had been waiting for this day to come, for he had planned it over the course of several weeks.

Well it didn't have to take several weeks, but he kept deciding yes but then no to this, and that was going back to Seattle and finding Hazel. She hadn't left her cell number anywhere for him but he knew where she lived, so that was a first.

He'd put his job on temporary leave (long vacation) in case anything happened and left his apartment vacant. It wasn't like he had that many things … just some clothes, the picture, car keys, and a few books. That was all he packed. The trunk wasn't even necessary, so all the items were put in the backseats of the car.

Cole ignited the engine, and off he went. He merged onto Highway Route 5 and raced down the road. The highway was a free place for him. He loved just riding between lanes every so often because it gave a sense of freedom to his consciousness.

It was a hundred miles to Seattle, so maybe a few hour drive.

Cole sped past towns and small cities, farmlands and suburbs. There was so much life around him, and he was only one of billions in the world. Everyone had a unique life, a different one, and he was only one of them. But yet, every one of them was precious.

There were a couple accidents which slowed traffic, but nothing too major or serious.

Just when everything seemed so boring, Cole saw the tip of the Space Needle. That meant Seattle was in sight. He gunned his engine and increased speed, eager to see Hazel again. "I'm not letting you down," he said to himself, though he was a bit nervous. "Whoever you've become, I'll still love you, and we'll finish the list of things you wanted to do with me. I repeat. We'll finish it."

Cole dreamed of her, how they got back together. He saw her in his dreams …beautiful as ever. Her beckoning him towards places …her hair flying in a swirl …her hand touching his. Cole wanted that back. He wanted to resume the relationship and mend the gaps that time and distance created between their love. He was going to make it right, and there was nothing that was going to stop him from doing so. Nothing.

But what would Hazel think of this … his actions? Leaving her?

He'd yet to know as he flew across the highway, straight to Seattle.

The wind helped. He'd opened the window to let the oxygen in, and it helped him. It boosted his confidence and as his hair flew about, it created a euphoric feeling in him.

He was going to undo the wrong. Be the hero.

Cole headed to Royal Plains, in the town of Oak Tails, just outside the city, and pulled out the exit. He was only several blocks away when he saw her there, on the side of the road.

Wait … was it really Hazel?

He looked closer, and he realized it was really her. He tried to motion something to her, but this complete act was enough for Cole to become so careless that he forgot he was driving through an intersection that had turned red and the other lanes turned green.

And with that, a Ford Ranger crashed right into his side. Boom!

The windows shattered, the sudden jolt pushed him into the steering wheel, and the force was enough to turn the car sideways onto the road. Cole had a split-second of realization before he was wiped-out from practically a combination of all of it.

Cole awoke, and he was standing up, except his eyes just opened. He registered everything immediately. He was in a wave and then his surfboard along with him flew out of the side. It was the same day at the beach, and he looked towards shore.

Hazel was clapping her hands and jumping, signaling to him how well he had done. He just slid through a wave.

Cole made his way back to the beach, and when he landed, Hazel ran to him and hugged him.

He was back, back where he belonged. But now he was having second thoughts. I thought I just crashed, Cole thought, but Hazel was so happy to see him that he decided to settle this later.

"Hey, you're really good at that, I love watching you," Hazel wrapped her arm through his arm and they scurried up to the boardwalk. Cole hesitated. This was super eccentric. He should be happy he was back, but it was the confusion of it all that still got him hanging. Hazel realized something was wrong, and she made it clear.

"Got something on your mind?" she asked.

Cole didn't want to lie anymore, even if she was not the same Hazel as the other Hazel, so he said "yes."

"Well, what are you waiting for … tell me!" Hazel demanded.

"Ok, but don't ask questions until the end … because this is going to sound really terribly confusing," Cole warned, and they sat on the sand together, facing the ocean.

Cole grabbed her hand and told her everything, and Hazel nodded after several phrases at a time while she traced shapes into the sand with the finger of her other hand. "There, I'm done, pretty crazy right," Cole concluded.

For a few seconds, Hazel didn't know what to say, but then she said, "I've been feeling something like that too."

Cole went all-out. "Wait so you were like me?"

"No, I mean, I can sense you in like another world ... another reality. You're not just here. You're over *there* too," Hazel responded. "Like no kidding, I think it's just we're so close to each other that I can recognize you over there. How am I over there?"

Cole pursed his lips. "You're exactly the same. You're cute, kind, helpful, very adorable, loving, especially adorable..."

Hazel blushed. "C'mon of course I'm adorable."

"Well, at least I'm back for now, so we can go back to our lives!" Cole brought up. "It's finally over …the nightmare."

"Was it really a nightmare? No right," Hazel pointed out.

"How …that's true," Cole admitted.

"I know you and I had a good time over there," Hazel smiled briefly.

"I had probably the two or three best days of my life over there," Cole explained.

"As a matter of fact, why did you leave me over there?" Hazel asked, her expression turned into a thinking one.

"I was lost, easy as that. I was just so lost," Cole proclaimed.

"It's okay. I know I forgave you. Here and there," Hazel told him.

"But how? You guys aren't even the same person…" Cole asked her.

"We're not, but we are. That's the simple definition," Hazel answered. "I'm sorry …some things don't have clear explanations that make much sense. Some things cannot be explained. For instance, love cannot be explained."

"You just have to live with it without ever really receiving an explanation. It's all about faith. Just accept it as it is," Hazel continued. "That's my life lesson to you."

"I can't do it," Cole told her. "I just can't."

"Then you should practice. That will do," Hazel told him and she rubbed her shoulders on his arm and nestled closer. "That's why I loved you, because I wanted to help you."

"And that's why I loved you, Hazel, because I wanted to be helped," Cole said, and they kissed each other.

The sky was a streak of dark blue with a hint of night showing, and the boardwalk lights had been turned on. It was much colder now, and the water was the prettiest it has ever been.

The kiss lasted for 10 seconds, and it was beautiful.

Hazel broke away half an inch away from Cole's face. She took a deep breath. "Remember what I told you? If we're ever separated for some reason, you're still my home and I am yours. Never forget this."

Cole nodded gingerly, his head slightly bent down, and they kissed once more, his arms around her back and her arms around his neck. The moment was unforgettable.

Side-by-side, they made their way up the beach onto the sidewalk. There were fewer people now since the sun was going down, and the sky streaked orange and yellow colors. Such a perfect instant, and Cole wanted to capture it and keep it forever. But they didn't bring a camera, and so the option was ruled out.

Cole was happy to be back, and Hazel surely was glowing. She was so understanding even when the situation showed otherwise. People say that in order to get to know somebody, you would have to spend a long time with them. But Hazel wasn't the same. She was always herself, and there weren't surprises. You could count on her, and Cole needed that. She was his lifeline. And Cole was Hazel's lifeline, for she couldn't lose him too. Cole, being the man, was determined to never let it occur, but who knows anymore since everything.

Hazel, on the other hand, took care of Cole as if he was a son. Cole loved the motherly aspect of Hazel, especially when she stroke him as they lay together. They would wrap up in a blanket and cuddle with each other once in a while. It was something they did on a regular basis for "fun" and because…well…they wanted to.

But Hazel needed Cole as much as he needed her. It was weird. From the moment they had met to now, every time they'd been together had flown past in a breeze. Not all the details for every reunion was recalled, but they still held on to one another. It was the history that was so strong, but again, the history didn't matter. They belonged with each other, and it was like the universe said so from the start.

Life wasn't in a rush. They strolled past little shops that sold souvenirs classified as beachy and also hermit crabs with painted shells of all sorts of designs. Even more, they passed hotels and restaurants on the right and the wide expanse of the beach to their left.

Some people were bicycling down the boardwalk and others were taking the "family bikes" which seated around four to six people. "We should do that one day," Hazel pointed to one. Cole didn't know if she hinted about a possible future where they had children …but he quickly cleared the thought and glanced elsewhere.

"You know, how is that I never really say anything meaningful, while you usually handle it," Cole exclaimed. Hazel peered at him. "What are you talking about …I'm jealous of everything that comes out of your mouth. Like it's really heart-touching."

"No …like why are you always saying the things that make me emotional and I'm just …really there," Cole asked. "Just stop …you actually confusing me so much. My living motto is this: Don't question, live. Get it?" Hazel raised her eyebrows.

"Alright, alright," Cole replied, but he did have something deep down inside he couldn't ignore. It was the fact that Hazel seemed to keep them going through speech and he barely contributed. She always said things that made him feel comfortable, but he decided that he did the same for her. For a guy, he thought it was his duty instead.

Hazel didn't seem to care much.

Hazel yawned. "I think we should head back."

"I'm hip," Cole responded, and they turned around and headed back the way they'd gone.

Reaching the car, Cole took the wheel and drove Hazel home. Seattle was still the same as the Seattle in the other reality. He passed by all the places he'd grown up knowing, and a sense of returning made him queasy. Hazel sat in the passenger seat, restless and quite tired. "I think I swam too much today."

"No, it's because I kept chasing you and you were trying to run around in water although you really cannot," Cole rolled his eyes. Hazel let out a laugh. "I admit this, I do."

Cole pulled up to her driveway and joked, "I don't think you'd like me to come in so much longer so ...I guess we're gonna have to call it a day on each other." Hazel played the scene. "Of course! Now I'm mad at you for making me so tired and you don't want me getting all over you ...nasty." "Yes, yes, I suppose I'll come by another day," Cole safely ended.

Hazel hopped out and went up to her door. She waved at him, and the sight of her made his heart drop. Hazel, Hazel, Hazel, he thought. Where would I be without you?

Surely the stars in the heavens put us together for a reason.

Cole was eager to see his apartment again, so he jacked up the engine of his car, which he was more than overwhelmed to see again, and skidded towards his own residence.

He stopped the car when he got there, and walked the flights of stairs that led to his apartment house. Cole was home. He found the keys and unlocked the door, opening slowly. The room was like how it was before, and it'd felt like a century.

Cole collapsed on his bed and touched his guitar tenderly, happy to feel the steel strings again.

What an adventure, he thought, but he knew the 2-3 days spent in the other reality would stay with him. He still wanted to know what happened, but not tonight. Tonight was for rest.

Slowly, as though he was on a boat in a calm sea careening back and forth, Cole drifted into sleep.

There he was, in the wave again. The flashes of his life shone before his eyes in an instant and then disappeared. The only difference this time was that the light that shone through the water came from the moon and not the sun. It was dark, and he was on the ocean.

Surely it was a dream, just a dream.

Cole was making his way through the wave, surfing the waters, and the end was right there, the aperture that led into the outside world not enclosed by the waters. He got ready to zip out and whip in a perpendicular angle to the shore.

Cole flew out and then he was falling in space, in darkness. His eyes couldn't register anything. He was falling too fast. His body was limp, and he couldn't move a single part.

Beep!

Cole arose and let out a huge breath. He was in a hospital bed and a nurse was beside him.

And then there was Hazel, sitting right there in front of him, tears in her eyes.

He was back in the second reality, and he remembered someone had crashed into him.

"Hey, how are you feeling," Hazel asked, her lip quivering. And then she broke apart.

"You have no clue! I was there, watching you see me before you got rammed into and then that was the worst instant of my life! I ran to you and I kept calling you up but you ignored me! WHY? WHY? WHY DID YOU IGNORE ME??? I THOUGHT YOU WERE GONE!" Hazel cried at him. "I couldn't let go of you."

Cole looked down, unsure of what to say. "I'm sorry," he replied honestly. "I really am. I'm sorry for making you feel that way. It was my fault," he continued.

It was so so bizarre. He'd just gone back to the reality he'd always known and now he was back here again. Could it get any worse? But he had a feeling that this time… he was going to be stuck here for a long time if not for good. It sucked.

"I can't lose you, Cole, I can't," Hazel struggled. "You're everything to me. You are."

To top that he'd just been whizzed back into what he thought was a parallel dimension or universe, he was faced with the difficulty of communicating to a teary Hazel. She was clearly traumatic and he had to settle things down before anything else.

"Hey Hazel, I just want to apologize. I'm sorry for leaving you even though we vowed to go through that list and be with each other forever. I promise to never do it again and I'll not leave your side," Cole promptly and controllably spoke.

"Can we resume everything the way it was before? And forget about the past?" Cole asked her.

Hazel wiped her face with her sleeve. Her eyes were all red and she had a frown on her. It hurt to see her like that, and Cole's heart broke at this. It was too sad.

Hazel nodded. "Ok," she slipped out. "I'm fine with that."

The nurse came in and told him, "You should be set to go in a few hours, just hang on."

Hazel and Cole sat in silence, sometimes staring at each other, and sometimes looking elsewhere. It was awkward but understandable. They haven't seen a long time, and it made perfect sense. Besides, they were going to hook back up on the right note.

"So ...how are you??" Cole inquired, breaking the silence.

"I'm well, how about you," Hazel said in a scholarly tone.

"I'm doing awesome! But I know you're doing awesome-er," Cole gave Hazel a heads-up.

Hazel giggled. "That's true. I *am* doing awesome-er."

She looked a little shy but flirty at the same time. Hazel kept glancing up and then down and she put both her arms on her lap. It looked like she was squeezing herself. "I mean you probably had the best time of your life when I wasn't there," Cole exclaimed.

"No, not true. You not being here equals me feeling …well not the same. No wait. Never-mind. You wanted me to say that. Forget what I said. I was having the time of my life, indeed," Hazel answered.

"Oh so me being here and me being not here doesn't make a difference?" Cole asked eagerly.

Hazel suddenly turned serious. "That's sensitive to talk about."

"Oh! My bad then. I meant that I brighten your day and you brighten mine …" Cole switched topics.

"Apparently yes," Hazel agreed.

"Nice seeing you again Hazel. For real."

"Nice seeing you too Cole …its great having you back," she pursed her lips dramatically and licked them.

Hazel batted her eyes.

"You haven't changed a bit since I saw you last time," Cole told her.

"Yeah, I did it for you. I wanted you to notice that," Hazel responded.

"So you were thinking of me the whole time," Cole inferred.

"Yes, that's correct Mr. Alessandro. I thought of you when I woke up, during the day, and before sleeping. I dreamt of the day you would come back and we can complete the list. On that day where we complete the list, something remarkable will happen," Hazel told him.

"And that is …?" Cole started.

"Oh, let's wait and see. Don't ask me! I don't know!" Hazel replied.

She was so sweet for who she was. It took a matter of hours until he could go. During the time, they had a conversation that brought them together again.

The nurse walked in.

"You're set to leave, but you're very lucky for not getting major injuries. However, you got minor wounds we stitched up already as you were passed out … so it's all good," the nurse informed him.

"Thank you so much," Cole told her. "I appreciate it."

He got discharged and sat up. Hazel came to his side and touched him lightly on the ribs. "So …let's roll?" she asked.

Cole nodded. "Yes, let's roll."

They strolled out of the room, got to the elevator, went down, and then emerged from the hospital. Hazel had her parked car in the parking lot and they got inside together. "I'm going to drive," she muttered to Cole and she fired the engine.

"Wait what …we're going right now?" Cole suddenly became aware.

"Of course! What'd you think? I planned that right when you got out of there we would continue completing the list …and only after that will I rest," Hazel responded like it was obvious.

"But …I just got in a crash, and I just left the hospital, and I need time to recuperate …" Cole trailed off. "I usually think for others …not this time. And you should partly blame yourself …several months late man," Hazel retorted. "Like what is that?"

"I'm done. I give up!" Cole surrendered, and Hazel laughed.

"I always win," she said.

"So …what is next on the list again? We finished like 2-3 things already right? So what's the fourth," Cole questioned.

"Well, you're going to my cabin in the woods halfway up a mountain. There's a lake there and you can do a lot. And there, we can finally be all alone, just you and me," Hazel put her arm around Cole as she drove with the other.

"Also, I forgot to say, you can camp there too. I heard that we will be able to see shooting stars there, and maybe even the northern lights. It will be so cool!" she added.

"I'm excited," Cole bounced back. "You're never tired."

"C'mon I thought you knew me. I obviously get tired, but when it comes to having fun …that's another story," Hazel explained. "And you, you're just an average boyfriend."

It was the first time Hazel had ever called him her boyfriend and Cole stuttered at this. From a very young age, he'd dreamed of the day Hazel would see him as her boyfriend, and that day had just come. "And you're a wild girlfriend," Cole joked back quickly.

"Like they say …wild and average make a good combo!" Hazel shrugged.

"I guess so," Cole agreed.

"We're heading into Canada," Hazel said.

"Wow really?" Cole asked.

"Yes really," Hazel confirmed.

"We going somewhere far?" Cole inquired.

"Stop asking too many questions …you'll see," Hazel replied.

First, Hazel took the highway. Then, she exited onto a smaller road and then an even smaller, more mountainous road. Finally, she pulled onto an unpaved gravel road. The ride was bumpy now, and Hazel and Cole kept hitting their heads on the roof.

They were reaching high altitudes. The air started getting misty and it was hard to see clearly through the path. Cole saw the wide expanse of land below in various spots. He could see towns as far away as the eye can see and even a far glimpse of Seattle. But it was mainly the amount of green he saw from above that overcame him with awe.

"Guess what? I brought my camera …can't not have that," Hazel spoke to Cole.

"Now we can take pictures …yay!" he answered dramatically.

They stopped at several overlooks and snapped a few images of each other. "I wish there were other people here to hold the camera because we can't be in together," Hazel said.

"We can take a selfie I mean …except it would be closer up," Cole responded.

"Yeah but then we look super weird," Hazel acknowledged.

"True," Cole agreed.

Hazel drove the car through an endless forest steadied on fluctuating slopes until at last Cole spotted a small two-story log cabin in the middle of nowhere, amidst a swarm of coniferous trees.

"Nice!" Cole exclaimed and he meant it.

"I knew you'd like it," Hazel cheered. "I knew it."

The cabin had a couple A-Frames up top and modern windows. There was a porch that extended around it, which gave the building a farmhouse touch to it. Some windows shaped as houses jutted out from the bent roof and gave a cap-cod feel. A chimney sat to the right made of stone and wooden stilts held up overhanging parts.

"This is yours? Like no kidding. It's yours?" Cole asked intently.

"Yeah! Who did you think it was?" Hazel asked rhetorically.

Hazel pulled up next to the house where the gravel road ended and stopped the engine.

"Trust me, inside is way better," she smiled.

"Can't wait," Cole said back.

She led him along a stone path to a wooden door. Taking out her keys, Hazel said,

"You'll never imagine what you're about to see." She unlocked the door and pushed in.

Cole walked into the most inviting place he'd ever been. The triangular roof allowed for so much empty space from the floor to the ceiling that it felt so airy. A fire was flickering in the grand fireplace and there were a few couches. A gigantic wool carpet covered the floor of the living room and a massive chandelier hung from atop. And it was warm too …so warm especially in the fall weather.

"I really like this," Cole seeming slipped out of his mouth.

Hazel was beaming. "Looks like I wasn't wrong when I said I would impress ya!"

"No you weren't," Cole concluded.

"We can do so much these three days! We can be off-the-grid and do fun stuff people with technology are missing out," Hazel explained. "Ok then," Cole replied.

"But first, I've been wanting to do this a long time," and Hazel suddenly grabbed onto Cole, urging his body to hers. Cole didn't get the message at first but then he understood.

Cole's blood was running.

Hazel led him to the couch next to the fireplace. It was so warm. So inviting. So pleasant. Cole took ahold of Hazel and took her down onto the couch. With his aid, Hazel tore off her shirt and her pants, only to reveal the inner clothing. Cole sat straight up and tore off his own shirt and lightly rubbed his lips over her belly-button and her chest. His head was in the clouds. Hazel seized this opportunity to roll Cole over onto the floor, where they kissed for a while as their bodies did the communicating. Cole clearly wanted this as much as Hazel did, and they'd finally did it. In a cabin. Somewhere far away. Somewhere distant.

That evening, they sat by the fire with each other, sharing a drink.

"Hey, do you want to camp tonight?" Cole asked her. Hazel replied, "Only if you want to."

"Maybe," Cole decided.

"Time to bring the photo albums out!" Hazel cried spontaneously. "And tomorrow, we can go to the lake a mile away and do some watersports there. There are people in that area so don't feel lonely. Besides, you got me …" and she snuggled even closer. Hazel stretched a hand out and slid a photo album of her into their arms. "So this is all about me…in case you didn't know."

Hazel opened up to the first page, and there were plastic slots where each picture resided. Cole recognized some of these but not all. There were pictures of her in different parts of the world, on trips, on research excursions, and many more.

She gave a short recount of every image, and a little background.

"So this one right here is when I went to the zoo and somehow all the seals kept following me in their pool to whichever part of the edge Hazel Francesca happened to be at," Hazel narrated. "That's because you're cute, so cute that seals like you too," Cole pointed out. Hazel glared at Cole, looking as though she wanted to slap him. "Shut up!" she laughed. "C'mon …are you not? Ok, I take that back," Cole retrieved.

"Wrong! You like me cuz I'm cute, so stop talking," Hazel declared. "Well, you are so ...it's not like I can resist you know," Cole conceded. "Of course, I'm a princess. No wait, a queen. Yes, I'm a queen, a really cute one," Hazel exclaimed.

"Your highness," Cole lay flat his palm.

"Anyway, let's continue." Hazel chatted about other photos as Cole listened and intervened frequently.

"Wait! We have to go see the northern lights, and there are supposed to be shooting stars tonight!" she cried after a moment.

"Let's hurry," Cole alarmed.

They got up and headed outside, to the car, and Hazel drove down to a plain circular field close to the cabin. It was dark now. "Should appear sometime tonight, who knows when," Hazel figured. "I really hope it's right now, but I'll go all night if we have to."

Hazel and Cole reclined on the grass, their arms stretched behind their backs as support. "I fit a blanket in the trunk, want to take it out?" Hazel asked him.

"Sure, if it's fine with you," Cole said. "I'll get it tho."

Cole walked over to the trunk and took the blanket out of it. He strode back and then lay it out on the bed of grass. "There, more comfortable."

"Thanks," Hazel cheeked.

They sat and waited, for minutes, then for hours. And then they saw the shooting star, flying across the sky. "There it goes!" Hazel admired. "It's so cool!" Cole acknowledged.

The star left a streak of light behind it, kind of like when jets leave a trail of steam behind to mark their paths, except this one was at night. In the dark-blue sky, the light was pretty.

And a few minutes later, the northern lights shone with great radiance. It was mystifying, each with their unique waviness and curvy pattern. "I never thought I would see this ... but now that I do, it's so beautiful," Hazel told Cole. "That's all I can say."

"I'm just at a loss for words," Cole agreed.

Cole grabbed Hazel's hand and they sat there, overcome by the overwhelming beauty of both the shooting star and the northern lights. "Nature is cute, everything is cute, you are cute," Hazel turned to Cole. He flashed a smile. "Yes I'm cute, but you are cuter."

Hazel grinned widely. "Love you man," she nudged him.

"I've got u girl," Cole replied. "Always."

And together, without needing a tent, they dozed off under the sky of dancing colors and light.

Cole woke first to the sound of insects chirping and birds singing. The morning dew had arrived. The sunlight radiated heat on his face. He slowly opened his eyes and saw everything before him. Trees towered around the circular field and the wind bent the grass.

Hazel had just woken up and was stretching her arms with her eyes closed. She opened them and cried, "Oh! You're awake? That was a good sleep ..." Cole answered, "I agree. Best of the best."

"I'll give it a 100," Hazel added.

"Didn't you want to go to the lake today?" Cole brought up.

Hazel looked up at him. "That's right! C'mon let's get moving."

"I helped you remember," Cole said proudly.

"I think I'm going to go wakeboarding, care to join?" Cole announced. "Well, I don't know if they'll let me hang onto you but if they do, hold me tight …" Hazel poked him. "Oh! I'll hold you so tight that there will be arm prints on you," Cole retorted. "Ok fine …not that tight," she gave Cole a dead stare.

Hazel gunned the engine and headed west towards a lake.

The car was parked on the side of the road and through the thick trees, Cole could see the vast blueness of the ocean surface. "Lakes are beasts," he muttered. "What was that? Oh yea, lakes are the best," Hazel nodded.

"I remember I went to a birthday party and you weren't there …and I got to dive into a lake and I didn't know what was in there but hey it was actually fun!" Cole exclaimed.

"Oh I wouldn't do that," Hazel replied. "Never."

They walked through the short forest into a clearing by the lake. There was a small dock there and they headed onto it.

"You sure?" Cole asked.

"I'm confused …sure about what," Hazel asked back.

"That you would never ever jump into a lake?" Cole answered.

"I said dive …ah!" Cole pushed Hazel into the lake and she fell in, made a decent splash, and re-emerged with her clothes all wet. "I am going to kill you Cole Alessandro. I will literally kill you," she said with a sneer, except it was obvious she was trying not to smile. "At least you got a free bath …" Cole responded.

"HEY! You got water in my nose and my mouth now I feel queasy," she retorted. "It wasn't me who pushed you …somebody else," Cole lifted his hands.

Hazel made a show of swinging her arm around. "Could there be possibly anyone else that could've pushed me? No," Hazel said. "They're hiding behind a tree," Cole told her.

"An actual person cannot run back down the dock to the woods before I got back to the surface. I would've seen it anyway…" Hazel argued drastically. "Only a tiger is that fast."

"It was a tiger," Cole responded. "A tiger, I repeat."

Hazel looked at him incredulous.

"Oh so you were the tiger right …cuz you're wearing an orange shirt with black stripes on it," Hazel observed.

Cole glanced down and was surprised.

"I AM wearing an orange shirt with black stripes. What a coincidence!" he cried.

Hazel replied, "You don't even know what you were …that's amazing. I know more about u than you do yourself."

"Isn't that how it works?" Cole approached her.

She thought for a moment. "That is true. Yup."

Hazel made her way to the shore. "Ouch! These rocks are killing my feet. They hurt so much."

"I can't believe you had the guts to push me and get me all wet. All your fault," she added.

"Proves that I'm capable of daring things," Cole retorted. "Easy."

"Thanks to you I feel so uncomfortable now," Hazel answered.

She made it to the shallow area and then slowly picked her way up to the grass. And right when she touched solid ground, Hazel came at Cole with full force and then tackled him. However, she forgot to stay balanced on the dock and her momentum carried both of them over the edge with Cole below her. "OH!" he said with a surprise.

Together, they tumbled into the water, and there was a gigantic splash.

Hazel came to the top first because she was less heavy and took a deep breath. Then, Cole rose to the top, his hair all wet. "Ha! Proves that I'm not afraid to retaliate …" she dug a finger into his cheek.

"What a baddie," he said. "You're such a baddie, doing that."

"At least we're even right now," Hazel replied confidently.

"I'm not going to start that ever again …this sucks," Cole told her. "I know it does, I just wanted to give you a taste of your own medicine …" Hazel flashed a smile.

"I'm all wet!" Cole cried.

"C'mon, let's go back to shore and dry ourselves," Hazel suggested. "Race you there. Last one is a rotten egg."

"O …" Cole was about to complain but Hazel had already taken off. "See you there!" she cried back.

Cole went in after her. "I'm going to get u."

Hazel swam as fast as she could while Cole went after her. Cole almost got his hand on her foot but she made a big splash and he was forced to stop for a moment because too much water had gotten into his eyes.

Hazel hit the shore, got up swiftly, and then started running along the edge of the lake. Cole made it and ran after her as though it was tag. She ran as though it was for her life and Cole picked up speed after her. And finally, Cole had caught up and he football-tackled her gently onto the grass. She yelped and giggled crazily.

"Nice catch!" Hazel complimented.

"Thank you," Cole answered. "Thank you very much!"

They broke apart and lay on the ground, looking up at the sky.

"Wakeboarding! Almost forgot!" Cole tapped Hazel's shoulder.

"Oh yea!" she scrambled up and then steadied herself for a second.

"Which way…Ms. Navigator?" Cole asked.

"Should be right. So this one," Hazel pointed to the right of her.

They trudged for a mile or two and then Hazel pointed across the lake to the other side where she said all the activities were. "We have to get there …by foot," she pointed out.

"Why didn't we just drive there?" Cole asked.

"Interesting. We could've. But I didn't want to. I wanted to enjoy the time with u walking. This is really the best part," Hazel retorted.

"I wish I could feel the same for u," Cole said.

"You already do. Everything you do shows that you do," Hazel assured him.

And then she spotted a small beach. "Let's skip rocks!"

"Ok," Cole shrugged.

Hazel went to the beach and started looking at the seashells on the sand. She picked up a flat rock and then threw it smoothly. The rock bounced once, then twice, then three times. "Woah! You're good. How do you do that? I can't," Cole asked her.

Cole tossed a rock and it fell in with a *droop* depressingly.

"Hey! Just keep practicing and trying. Here ...let me help you," and so Hazel took on the task of teaching him.

"So, you find a good rock first. I usually like flat, medium-sized smaller ones," she started.

Cole scanned the area next to his feet and picked up a good rock, one that fit Hazel's criteria.

"Ok now you need to have a good stance. So one foot forward and the other back. And then you swing your hand back and then you throw the rock like a Frisbee … at least that's how I do it. So it's all about the follow-through too. Oh yea! I more thing. The flick of the wrist is important too. It should be quick and natural," Hazel told him.

"Ok, I'm going to try …" Cole said.

He did exactly what Hazel said but was hesitant so he didn't put enough power.

"Perfect! Except you need more power in it," Hazel saw.

"Got it," and Cole tried again, striking a perfect quadruple splash.

"You're a fast learner!" Hazel exclaimed. "That's striking."

"No … it's because I had a good teacher," Cole pointed at her.

"Thank you … I like how we're appreciating each other so much."

"You're welcome … or should I say no problem?"

"Either or both."

Cole and Hazel continued the trek to the other side of the lake, chatting about really anything that came to their minds. At last, they were close. "We're almost there!" Hazel observed with a hand shielding the sun from her face.

They came to a section where the lake flowed into a small creek. There was a log that lay across it, and it was the only path to get across without getting wet again. However, there were also stepping rocks in the water that had exposed surfaces to stand on.

"Seriously?" Cole complained.

"I'm taking the stepping stones way … don't know about you," Hazel announced.

"I'm going to take the log," Cole countered.

As though it was a balance beam, Cole stepped across the log heel on toes and repeat. Hazel got to the other side quicker and was making fun of him being slow. "I didn't even get wet this time!" she mocked. "Thanks for making me feel miserable," Cole replied sarcastically.

After 20 more minutes of trudging in the woods, they'd made it into a clearing where an old one-stall wooden shack stood next to the lake. Cole went up to the square opening he could peer inside and then leaned onto the table there.

"Hello?"

Silence.

"Hello?"

A surfer guy with long, curly hair and a rock-star appearance popped up to the counter. He had one of those shirts that only covered his body and a trunk on. In addition, the dude had a pair of sunglasses on and a stern countenance.

"Good day brah, what can I help you with?" and then he spotted Hazel coming behind Cole, and he suddenly found himself staring at her. Cole attempted to return his attention. He waved his hands in front of his face, and the dude blinked a couple times and then shook his head. "Oh sorry, but I've just gotta be honest …your girlfriend's kinda hot," he said, "but it's not like I want her …no that's the wrong idea …just saying she's a hot one." Cole nodded, "I get it, it's okay."

"Alright, I'm just tryna take a wakeboarding ride with my girl," Cole told him. "Oh we got those! Ok man, meet me at the lake edge in 10 minutes while I get ready," the man said.

There were some other people there, but it wasn't overly populated. Some went tubing, and others went paddle-boarding. And even more people were tanning under the sun and enjoying the fall weather by the lakefront.

"The guy said I was hot?" Hazel asked Cole. "Yeah," he responded. She blushed, "I turn heads man. Boys' heads."

Cole remembered back in middle school and high school when all the boys were falling for Hazel. Cole wasn't the most popular kid but he was high up there somewhere. Although many guys chased Hazel with all their might, she kept moving closer to Cole. The more the boys tried to get her, the faster she attached to Cole, and he never really understood why. Hazel liked him more, and why was that?

They sat under the shade against a tree trunk as the surfer guy prepared everything.

Hazel sighed. "You ready for this? You seem nervous, I can feel it."

Cole found himself trembling.

"How am I anxious? This isn't even scary or hard ..."

"Because you've never done it? Mm hmm I know it," Hazel said.

"You can read my mind!" Cole exclaimed.

"I can, yes, I can," Hazel nodded sleazily.

"And ...you're a terrible liar, so bad at it. I can do so much better ..." Hazel nudged his arm.

"I'm sure you can," Cole agreed.

"So I'm guessing it's not me who's going to be hanging onto you …it's you that's going to be hanging on to me?" Hazel asked, an eyebrow raised. "What …no!" Cole cried.

"That's what I thought …let's see about that," Hazel challenged.

Cole led Hazel to the lakefront where the surfer guy was fixing the string to the rear of the boat that was going to take them around. The man tinkered with several things and then said, "All set …though I need to give some rules."

"Rule number one: Please keep both hands on the triangular handle right here …at all times," he pointed to the end of the string opposite of the boat where there was indeed a handle in the shape of a triangle. "Rule number two: Try not to fall into the water."

Hazel gulped. "Ok then."

The surfer guy hopped into his boat and Cole bent down and lifted the rope that connected the handle with the vehicle. Hazel wrapped her arms around his middle. "Can't believe we're doing this," she looked up to him. "I know right!" he replied.

The boat slowly moved from the lakefront into the emptiness of the water followed by the rope and then Hazel and Cole sliding down the dirt onto the water. "Here goes nothing," Cole shrugged.

Next, the boat turned a sharp right and started speeding up like an airplane on a runway. The board they stood on slid through the water and kept increasing quickness.

And just a short time after, the board was so fast that water was jetting out from the sides and spraying them and their life jackets. They screamed together joyfully while trying to maintain balance.

Cole never thought skating on water was so fun. Hazel and he were swung from side to side uncontrollably as the boat moved in the directions it went. "This has to be the craziest thing I've done in my life!" she cried. "So true," Cole shouted back.

The wind blew past them, and the water splashed them from every angle. It was hard seeing the landscapes around the lake because of the thrill they were experiencing. Hazel and Cole were in the middle of the lake, spinning in every way.

Hazel bent down and took a handful of water, splashing Cole. He immediately recoiled from the coldness and sought revenge. "I'm going to get you back ...you know that."

Cole squatted and took his share of water, and throwing it onto Hazel, who yelped in fear and looked the other side. She jerked up as the liquid touched her skin. "That's cold!"

"That's what you did to me ...so," Cole widened his eyes.

"Not cool," she shook her head and then sneered. "What if I just pushed you off right now?"

"No ...you absolutely wouldn't. No," Cole shook his head.

"Watch me," she warned and slammed into Cole with such a force that knocked him off-balance and sent him side-first into the water with Hazel on top. One moment he was breathing fresh air ....the next he was submerged into a lake, choking on water.

Hazel held onto him the whole time, so it was effort to get to the surface. When they did, Cole was gasping for air desperately as though it was running out. "No ... you didn't do that."

"Yes I did, and I'm proud of it," Hazel eyed Cole.

The surfer guy thought they were still on the board so the boat kept going, farther away into another section of the lake.

"Let's swim back to shore and escape before he finds us ... then we can pass paying for a ride," Hazel suggested, and Cole said why not.

They swam together to the edge of the lake and then crawled out.

"Swimming gets you hungry ... we should go ... I know a place we could go to," Hazel pointed out.

"That's a dead move ..." Cole urged.

They hurried into the thickness of the trees and resided there for a while, taking a break. From there, Cole and Hazel made it all the way back to her car and drove out.

She pursed her lips. "That was fun I guess."

"Good time …I'd say," Cole corroborated.

Hazel checked a smile. Cole loved watching her do simple stuff like driving the car. She was so natural at it.

"There's a steakhouse on the side of the road somewhere, can you help me find it? It should be up ahead," Hazel brought up.

"There! I see it! Right there!" Cole showed her a building that was coming up.

She pulled into the parking lot and stopped the car.

"You know this place?" Cole asked her.

"Yeah, used to be one of my childhood favorites, in case you didn't know …" Hazel told him.

"A steakhouse? I never expected that…" Cole seemed intrigued.

"You're not the first, but yeah," Hazel answered.

The steakhouse had the making of a log cabin. All its support beams were logs as well as the walls.

"That's pretty *loggy,*" Cole observed. Hazel slightly nodded her head.

She opened her car-seat door and burst out, prompting Cole to do the same as he studied what was in front of him. The steakhouse was large, and behind it was a wide expanse of land that sloped down. An entire valley stood below.

"C'mon let's go in ...I'm so hungry I could eat you," Hazel addressed Cole. "Not kidding," she added.

Cole grimaced, but didn't say anything.

Hazel got to the door and put her hand on a straight wooden bar that was the handle.

With all her effort, she pulled and went in along with Cole. There were a set of double doors, so Hazel had to do it a second time.

"Work those muscles girl! C'mon ..." Cole cheered.

"Not helping," Hazel uttered back through the side of her lips.

And then they were in, and Cole was swept by the magnificent character of the steakhouse.

It was grandeur, and also dark. The walls were made of black planks and lined with antiques. It was also open-concept with booths on the sides as well as short and long tables occupying the middle. All the waiters and waitresses were dressed in long, white uniforms and displayed supreme, positive attitudes to their guests.

"You never told me ..." Cole trailed off because a waiter had interrupted them.

"Good evening couple ... would you prefer a table or a booth?" the waiter asked. He had a bushy mustache and a tint of a European accent to his voice. His head was mostly bald and his stomach wide. Cole wondered how being a waiter wasn't enough exercise, but he dismissed this with the belief that some people are larger through birth and genetics. As they say, everyone is different.

"Table please ..." Hazel replied quickly.

"Spectacular ... off this way please..." he grabbed two menus and lead them to their table. Cole could see the distant sunlight peeking through the windows on the other side, and then he realized he and Hazel were actually going to be sitting at the back of the steakhouse where the scenery was prime.

The waiter stopped at a table next to the window and said, "Enjoy your meal, your server will be here in a minute ..." Hazel responded, "Thank you."

There was a candle in the middle and adequate accessories. The knife and the fork lay next to one another as well as a spoon for soup on the opposite side of the plate. The plates were decorated with what looked like cave paintings and patterns of colors involving stripes and much more. Through the light of the fire in the candle, Hazel's eyes glinted and her face illuminated.

"You look so nice right now ... as a side note," Cole complimented.

"I knew you'd say that! So do you ... this makes you look a whole lot better. Before, without this fancy setting, you'd look super not so nice ..." Hazel answered sarcastically.

"Thanks a lot," Cole replied.

The new waiter arrived and introduced himself. "Hi how are you guys? My name is

James Charles and I'll be your server today. Can I start y'all with some drinks?"

"Water with lemon? Yeah," Hazel told him.

"How about water *without* lemon for me," Cole looked up to the waiter.

"No problem … I'll be back on my way … just let me know when y'all are ready to order," James Charles said.

"Of course!" Hazel cheered.

"To be honest, I've only been here a few times … so not that much. I said it was one of my childhood favorites and indeed it was … but I mean, we didn't come so much … my parents plus me and my brother. We came half of the time when we were here. Otherwise, we'd be back in old Seattle … living it up," Hazel informed him.

"When I was a kid, my parents would bring me to fast-food chains and call it a day …" Cole retorted. "That's how we lived it up back then. Just like that …"

Hazel let loose a small laugh.

"But you're so fit …so how …?" she questioned.

"I don't even know …" Cole thought for a second.

The waters came, and Hazel requested a toast, so they chinked their glasses while holding them.

Hazel basically chugged the glass of water down to the lemon, ice and all. "Dang …you're thirsty," Cole acknowledged.

"You're so right. I *am* thirsty. But not just that. I'm *desperately* thirsty. Who knew being in water actually drains your water?" Hazel spoke.

"Not me …" Cole said.

"Uh Mr. James Charles? I think she needs some more water …" Cole called, and then said to Hazel, "Here …take mine first …and I'll take yours."

"Aw …such a gentleman. I dig you for that," she pretended to react to something adorable.

Cole smiled. "That's what I do …gotta always be there for you."

"Honestly ...why boast even?" Hazel switched gears.

"Always in for the appreciation. I have to make that last ...it's a matter of feeling good about yourself," Cole shrugged.

"If you weren't you ...I would mind. But since you ARE you ...I wouldn't mind. Congratulations Cole Alessandro. You passed the FIT-ness test. Ha ...get it?" Hazel slapped herself, pretending to throw her head back and start a laughing act.

"That was cringey ...please don't do that again. It messes up that perfect picture of you in my brain ..." Cole joked. "I don't feel so well now," he continued to play.

Hazel stopped laughing. "Ok, ok."

"Let's play the staring game ...where we just stare at each other and try to guess what the other person is thinking. In the meanwhile, under the table, we can trace each other's legs with hints ...but here's the catch...only pictures and no words," Hazel suggested.

"Sounds good, let's do it," Cole agreed. He bore his eyes into hers while she did the same back. It was hard looking at her eyes

…they were just shining and so brilliant. He loved the game, really because it gave an excuse for eye-contact awkwardness.

And after a couple minutes, Hazel started making faces to Cole and tilting her head slightly to the right first and then the left. Cole returned his own expressions as surprise ones or confused ones. He wondered how they would be if they starred in a movie together.

"Hey cutie …" Cole slipped out of his mouth.

Hazel sat straight up, alarmed. "Don't you call me that again! So rude!" she projected.

"Woah! I thought you'd like it," Cole raised his hands innocently. "Now I know the truth …" he grinded his white teeth.

"Just kidding … it ain't that bad … just unexpected … and apparently radical coming from a guy like u. When guys call me nicknames … I tend to favor the more mellow ones … so be on the lookout," Hazel contracted her eyebrows and batted her eyes.

"I got it. Won't make the same mistake again … promise ya," Cole pointed at her. They continued to look at each other. Cole thought of what she thought of him, and Hazel thought of what he thought of her. Their connection was so strong.

"Did you just realize this is kinda the first date we're having? Like a real one …" Hazel brought up.

"Oh yea! Never thought about that … but you're right," Cole shot back.

"Just two young people on a date … ain't it nice?" Hazel said dreamily to herself. Cole replied, "I like this, I really do."

"Back to the food!" Hazel suddenly snapped. "Geez, I don't know what I'm getting …"

"Get seafood … always the best," Cole suggested.

"This is a steakhouse!" Hazel looked at him and blinked a few times as though she couldn't underestimate what he just said.

"Yeah but my philosophy is that you shouldn't order something that they claim to specialize in but rather take something you know you probably already like," Cole explained.

"I like taking risks, so no thank u," Hazel pounded the table.

"I mean …is it worth it to try? I'm not sure …that choice is on you," Cole shrugged.

"Oh! Let's get chips and spinach dip …that sounds so good!" Hazel pointed at the menu.

"Whatever …I'm really fine with anything," Cole resided.

"That's what they all say," she rolled her eyes, "Can't you be the least different? Huh?"

"Maybe, but I don't want to in front of you," Cole looked aside. "What about you though?"

"Oh me? Easy. I don't gotta be nervous when I'm there with you," Hazel retorted.

"Big facts!" Cole said sarcastically. "I totally believe you."

"We should stop flirting and get things going. This is the reason why we never get anything done," Hazel exclaimed.

"Honestly …what are these things we have to get done?" Cole questioned.

Hazel contemplated for a second.

Cole contracted a smile. "Nothing …correct?"

Hazel thought for a moment more. "Well, not necessarily."

"Oh so that's a yes …ok I see now," Cole looked down.

"Whatever. Hurry up and help me decide!" Hazel urged frantically.

"Give me that," Cole took Hazel's menu.

"You legit have one in front of you …what is this?" she asked.

"Well yours is different because you looked at it …there," Cole justified.

"You don't make *any* sense, I'm sorry to say, but this is not a false claim mister," Hazel put her hands on her hips. "So are you going to help me or what man?"

Cole pondered quickly. "Yeah sure, this one time!"

"Wow, such a great guy …" Hazel replied sarcastically. "Guaranteed always be there for me …will actually help me …uh keep me company …uh just be that awesome, spectacular dude everyone loves …totally."

"I would love to hear you rant …but I gotta concentrate on tryna find you the perfect dish…so quit it!" Cole demanded.

"Ha ha so funny …no! Once I get turned on …it takes me a while to turn off …u know what I'm saying," Hazel responded.

"No …I don't know what you're saying," Cole answered.

"Seriously? I thought you had an above-Einstein IQ! I guess I'll just tell you anyway. So basically …you know what? I'm going to let you figure it out all on your own …cuz you're so good right?" Hazel pointed out.

"Challenge accepted. Gonna figure it out all by myself …absolutely no help from anyone at all!" Cole retorted.

"Ok. Coolio cheerios," Hazel said.

"Wait what? What is that supposed to mean?" Cole inquired.

"It translates to 'we have a deal.' You didn't know?" she asked.

"I have never heard you say that," Cole told her.

"Well now you know. It's our secret language," Hazel kicked him from beneath the table.

"Ow! That hurt," Cole reacted. "I'm going to kick you back harder."

"Not if I get you first!" Hazel kicked with both legs at Cole's legs and he howled in pain to the point he almost fell out of his seat onto the floor. "You're paying for this," he warned.

"Oh is that a threat? Bring it," Hazel played him.

"We're officially at war you know," Cole pointed out. "No mercy."

"I can single-handedly wrestle you to the floor if I had to, but not right now. We're in a restaurant, it ain't gonna work this way," Hazel said. "Otherwise, I would destroy you."

"Such an aggressive person ... dang," Cole glanced at her.

"Always gotta be looking tough and tryna seek a fight …that's really something there. I admire you for that," Cole nodded. "Well very soon you'll be wishing you hadn't," Hazel responded. "C'mon I can't even act nice towards you anymore? I give up. Actually," Cole relaxed. "No it's because it wasn't genuine …you see? I can tell," Hazel fired back. "Ok then, if it gotta be like this then it gotta be like this."

"Such a nice pickup line, I applaud you. Bravo!" Hazel clapped silently.

"Shut …" Cole sighed.

"You have to play it cool around me or else I won't see you in a grand light so please …" Hazel told him.

"I'm doing my best …" Cole assured her.

"Well your best is not enough. Even better! Jump for that goal!" Hazel encouraged him.

"Ok," Cole let loose a breath of air.

Cole liked that about Hazel. She was very cute in her own way but she could be fire at times. And in contrast, Hazel loved Cole for being the guy who was very chill but could still have fun simultaneously.

The waiter arrived at their table.

"All set? Or do y'all still need some time," James Charles asked.

Cole looked at Hazel.

"Yeah, I think we're good," he said.

Cole motioned, "I'll go first."

As he ordered, Hazel started smiling at first and then giggling. Cole saw this and he found himself smiling too.

"What's so funny?" James Charles the waiter asked curiously.

"I don't even know bro …ask the girl," Cole elbowed him.

"Nothing …it's just him," she pointed back at Cole.

"Me?" Cole asked.

"Yeah, it's just you're funny …being yourself. I know it's kinda weird but yes. You yourself is funny," Hazel worked hard to suppress the growing, ever-expanding smile on her face.

"Ok …well keeping that in mind …it's your turn!"

Hazel looked at the menu.

"Hey James Charles …got any recommendations?" she asked.

Cole slapped his face. "R u …"

"Shh, let the girl talk," James Charles the waiter said to Cole. "Go on."

As a side note, Cole recalled the time they went to watch a movie that was about …you guessed it …a guy and a girl. In sum, the guy and girl liked each other but they were too afraid to show it so they passed their time dating other people. But in the end, after all the failed attempts, they realized they were each other's destiny.

James Charles addressed Hazel, "I personally really like the pasta. Get the pasta with shrimp and a slice of sirloin steak. That has gotta be one of my mains here …"

Hazel replied, "Bet, let's do it."

"As normal, I would've ordered what the girl ordered but I really believe that the steak with fries and mashed potatoes is way better than you know ...that," Cole joked.

"He's lying ...don't trust a thing he says ...just don't," Hazel told James Charles. "I'm not playing."

James Charles made a show of calming. "Ok, ok, I guess I can't trust neither of you now ...!"

"Good idea, please do," Cole pointed out.

"He's right this time. You can trust that," Hazel jutted a thumb at him.

James Charles went away smiling.

"Good work, we just creeped out a waiter at some restaurant," Hazel extended her arm and patted Cole's shoulder.

"Honestly, I think we freaked him out. We go team!" Cole nodded.

"Most *eccentric* couple in the universe! We can actually win that title," Hazel brought up. "Easily."

"But other people who are competing for the same title have been training their whole life!" Cole retorted.

"But we're so nice at this that we don't need training. It's in our element," Hazel shot back.

"True, can't deny that," Cole agreed.

"Ok, let's just enjoy the rest of lunch plz. Could use some quiet time for both of us ..." Hazel urged.

"You're right! Fat bet ... I'm good to go don't know about you," Cole raised his eyebrows.

"Always a step ahead of you bro," Hazel retorted smartly.

"Ok ... you're a G ... I see," Cole raised his hands to his chest.

"Of course! And you always below me no matter ..." Hazel replied.

"Good. Deal. Whatever ... speaking to you is a waste of saliva," Cole explained.

"For you maybe not. I know you loveeee talking to me! Cuz no other girl is gonna listen to you babbling off ..." Hazel dramatized.

"I've gotta admit that for once!" Cole nodded.

"C'mon let's have a good meal before we go …" Hazel turned away smiling.

"Yeah, let's do it," Cole concluded.

***

The lunch was probably one of the best Cole had ever had. The steak especially was perfection at its finest as well as the mashed potatoes. Hazel asked him for a little to "try."

In return, Cole asked for a bit of hers, and she was like "go ahead!" It turned out that Hazel's plate was so much better than his.

"Why is yours so good?" Cole had asked.

And she was like, "Cuz I know how to choose food at a restaurant unlike somebody else …" she then shrugged.

Now they were on the road again … heading back to the cabin.

"You in for something not as active as wakeboarding?" Hazel asked out of the blue.

"Huh? Oh yes … yes," Cole answered.

"What should we do then?" she pressed her cheek together and glanced at Cole as she drove.

"Something that's not wakeboarding," Cole responded.

"Seriously dude. And we're leaving by late afternoon …we're heading towards Seattle cuz we got a concert to catch at 7:30 pm so we must savor the last moments here …" Hazel sounded intimidating.

"Ok, give me a sec," Cole put up a hand.

What could they do honestly?

"We should just play cards …go classic u know," Cole suggested.

Hazel thought for a while. "Sure."

She drove the car up the smaller road towards the cabin. There, from behind the thickness of the coniferous trees, a wooden structure came into view and stood solid as ever.

"I'm actually falling in love with this place," Cole told Hazel.

"See? I knew it. You loved this place from the very beginning."

"I'm amazed at how well you know me …"

"Don't be. I was meant to," Hazel resorted. "The way you say it is like a happy ending," Cole said. "It's really how you look at it. It can always be happy if you want it to be," Hazel replied.

"Elaborate," Cole responded.

"It doesn't have to be a sad ending unless you let it be. It can always be happy …positive," Hazel cheered.

Cole casually and slowly nodded because he only half got it.

"Never mind, it isn't really that important …but hey …we're about to play cards!" Hazel switched topics.

"This is gonna be super fun," Cole exclaimed.

Hazel parked the car in the driveway and she led Cole through the path to the front door. Then, with trembling and excited hands, she lifted her keys from her pockets and opened the door.

Cole scrambled in and then a question popped into his head.

"Um Hazel ... where are the cards at?"

Hazel grinned at him frivolously. "Let me handle that ... you sit on the couch and wait."

Cole walked out of her way and headed to window to look out. As he daydreamed for a tad, Hazel surprised him from behind saying, "All set ... are you playing or what?"

He dropped onto the couch next to Hazel as she shuffled the cards.

"How do you do that? Like the shuffling. I've always tried but no luck," Cole motioned to the cards.

"Let me show you then," Hazel turned to him and changed her seating. She had crossed-leg with socks off. "U know what? C'mon let's sit on the carpet ... that'd be better."

"Sure," Cole agreed.

They relocated down, and then Hazel got all into business.

"So first, you make sure all your cards are back-to-back, so basically just set ur deck on the ground then they'll be even. And then you peel off from the middle out so that you have two halves, one on either hand. Then, you put your thumb on top of each group of cards and ur middle finger underneath with your pointer finger as support. From there, you just slowly release the cards."

"Only one problem … I've done the exact procedure so many times and it doesn't seem to work for me," Cole intervened.

"I'm guessing the cards don't like you," Hazel told him.

"Probably. Just might be the reason," Cole thought.

Hazel continued shuffling for a few more times before distributing the cards into piles.

"Which game are we playing?" Cole asked.

"Go Fish. Always gotta start classic right? Wasn't that what you said?" Hazel asked like she wanted to know the answer although it was clear she already knew.

"Don't tell me you don't know how to play," Hazel looked up at him.

"No I know how to play ... totally," Cole said although he really didn't.

"Yea ... you don't," Hazel observed.

Cole practically jumped up on the couch.

"Did you just read my mind ... again?" he exclaimed suddenly.

"It's really not that hard with you cuz you make it so apparent," Hazel laughed. "Really easy in fact."

"I've gotta try harder now. Oh watch me. I'll make it so hard you won't even know it," Cole pursed his lips.

"Challenge me, I dare. Do it. Bring it," she answered.

Hazel resumed what she had been doing. "Ugh, we just wasted some time talking about non-important things ..."

She quickly dealt Cole seven cards and also set aside seven for herself beside her lap.

"Remind me ... uh how do we play?" Cole tensed, expecting an outrage from Hazel.

"C'mon, are you that afraid of me? Tell me, am I intimidating?" she asked earnestly.

"Oh yea," Cole said in a deep, urging voice. "No doubt."

"Um, yes!" Cole shot back.

Hazel gave him a big smile with her eyes squinted. "Thank u."

"Let's start the game before we forget all about it," Hazel immediately suggested.

"Good point," Cole nodded.

She picked up her seven cards and held it like a fan and Cole copied her and tried to do it secretly so it wouldn't be embarrassing if Hazel found out he was watching her every move to imitate. "You think ur stealthy?" Hazel laughed, "But I'm sorry …you're not."

"C'mon u gotta bring me down like that? I'm practicing!" Cole retorted smartly. "No …you're performing when you're in front of me …so try practicing on other people …that's really what u thinking," Hazel lifted her head. "In short, I speak truth."

Hazel spoke, "So this is what u do, and I'm only saying it once. You see if you have pairs and then you take them out. And then we ask each other for cards and go back and forth until one of us gets a card with the same number for every card we have and whoever that is wins."

"That's awfully complicated," Cole shook.

Hazel slapped her face. "You're so annoying some times," she muttered.

"Hey, but remember, I'm always trying my best," Cole pointed out.

"Let's do a test round …okay?" Hazel asked. "Is that too much to ask?" she added with a glint in her eyes.

"Sounds like an awesome plan …let's roll," Cole shrugged.

Hazel started and took out her pairs. Cole copied her as usual.

As she took out her pairs of kings and fives, Cole took out a queen and four at the same time.

"No! You match the numbers on top at the corner of the cards!" Hazel exclaimed. "Looks like u need a lot of help."

"But they're the same color! And the same shape!" Cole argued.

"Numbers bro …numbers. Please tell me u know what numbers are," Hazel repeated.

"Yea, but a queen isn't a number," Cole answered.

Hazel bit the insides of her cheek. "Treat it like a number."

Cole pursed his lips, "Ok, I can do that."

Hazel asked him, "Do you have a ten?" Cole took a swift glance at his cards, "Nah, I don't."

"Do you actually don't," Hazel questioned skeptically.

"For real," Cole backed himself up.

Hazel reached for his cards suddenly and Cole reacted with fear in his eyes and also his free hand stretched out to grab Hazel's. In return, Hazel reacted with her own fear and she dove right into Cole. They rolled over onto the floor below the couch on their backs together.

She was laughing, so was he. "Why do we do this all the time? Like it's really for no reason," Hazel asked, her eyes stunningly watching Cole. In response, he flashed a quick smile.

"I guess that's just how we roll ... right?" he concluded.

"Makes sense," Hazel tapped her cheek. "It does."

She drummed on Cole's hand while they lay there for a while looking up through the skylight that was really high in the air. Nothing. They were doing nothing, and there didn't seem to be anything going on around them. This was the best life can get.

Cole remembered times when he'd heard people tell him to take life easy. His elementary school bus driver always said, "You might get disappointed ... but keep the joy in you ... don't forget." The driver was always such a great guy who liked to engage with the children and support them if they needed it.

Hazel sat up and took her pile of cards.

"Ok, starting off from where we were …by the way, we're leaving in a couple hours …" Hazel gave a heads-up.

Cole got the hang of it. Hazel knew when he was having trouble so she would scoot over and teach him.

"So you put these two together cuz they are the same and then you can just drop them on the ground …it doesn't really matter if I see them anymore," she explained.

"Wow …I'm so bad at this …thanks Hazel," Cole responded.

Before long, Cole was rocking it. They had made it through a few rounds of Go Fish already and he'd won three out of four of them. "I'm proud of you …keep it up," Hazel observed.

"C'mon you should start winning …don't let me get all the dubs," Cole told her.

"What if I want u to get the dubs instead?" Hazel asked.

"Then I wouldn't want u to want me to get the dubs," Cole replied.

"Logical," Hazel shrugged.

By the sixth round, Cole called, "Last pair!" and he dropped his two cards and exclaimed, "I won."

Hazel melodramatically dropped her own cards and said, "I quit."

"I thought you were more relentless than that," Cole told her.

"You just won every round except the first ... I'm kinda shaken," she replied. "Just a tad."

"Ok then ... I'll let u win the next one ... and I'll still *try* to beat u ... what about that?" Cole cheered.

"Nah, it's okay," Hazel pursed her lips.

She checked the clock on the wall. "We better start packing! We got a concert to make."

"Right on," Cole bolted up.

They loaded the limited things they'd bring from Seattle into the car and Hazel ignited the engine.

"It's gonna be a 2 hour drive so buckle up!" she cried.

After they said goodbye to the cabin (which Hazel said they would come back to in the future), Hazel drove the car down the same small road into a larger road down the mountain and through valleys. The space around them was vast and charming.

"Someday, I might buy a house here …just for the view and the nature," Hazel said.

"So you're gonna leave me?" Cole joked.

"Oh no …definitely not. You're coming with me. It's an order," Hazel corrected herself.

"I'm never leaving u out of my sight for longer than a day," she added.

"Neither will I do the same for u," Cole acknowledged.

He kissed her almost spontaneously, but their lips connected at the right moment, and it was vibrant.

It was only a second long, but it got Hazel in a much better mood to drive. "Isn't it tiring to drive for so long at a time?" Cole asked her. Hazel turned her head to him.

"No, not when the best guy in the world is sitting approximately 6 inches away from you," Hazel answered.

Cole nodded understanding.

"Legit, you making this list of activities …don't you ever get tired of fun? Like it's so weird. Everything we do is basically for fun, so do u think it's right to just have fun the rest of your life?" Cole asked her. Hazel grinned. "I don't know about everyone else, but in my book …yes. I wish to have fun all the days I'll ever have."

"I admire your positivity," Cole lightly pinched Hazel.

"Yup. And I admire you for your curiosity," Hazel retorted.

"So tell me, what's this concert we're going to?" Cole inquired.

"Oh, you'll love it. You know her …and she's also so pretty. Do you know Andrea Paige? Her vocals are *so* nice," Hazel said. Cole knew her, she was always a favorite of Hazel.

"C'mon you've gotta say she's kinda cute," Hazel nudged Cole. "Even I'm a girl and

I sort of like her. Like you're a guy …and there's not a guy who doesn't have a crush for that girl. But frankly, I think I'm nicer-looking …" she put out.

"You're not wrong on that one," Cole pointed out.

"Hey, wanna listen to one of her tracks? I got a complete disc of three of her newest albums right here," Hazel brought up.

"Sure," Cole said, because he didn't know what else to say.

Hazel took one hand and reached into the box between their seats.

"I got it, just tell me the name," Cole volunteered.

"Ok, yea, so it's Summer Mist, and it's so good," Hazel responded.

Cole peered around for a bit until he spotted the words 'Summer Mist' and then he pulled it out.

Then, Cole opened the cd box and then slid the disc into the music player above.

There were a few clicks and then the music started playing, and Cole recognized the instrument, an acoustic guitar.

Even more, however, Cole realized Hazel's abrupt shift in character.

She was singing, and her voice was beyond beautiful. Not only did it match the voice of the singer, but it also went to a higher level than that, one that shone with more elegance and power. Her motions too. She was swinging her hair around, winking, rolling her shoulders, and it was crazy. Cole sat there watching her, hearts in his eyes.

"We be out here spinning in circles, dashing our hurdles

I can't explain how we connect so well

But what I do know is this one thing

And that is, we were made for each other ..."

She was so exciting always ... always tryna get the best out of everything, and it was spectacular seeing her like this.

After the first verse and the chorus, Cole decided to give it a try and join in with her.

He started singing alongside Hazel, and she didn't seem to realize, or maybe she did but chose not to interrupt the vibe.

She sang soprano, he sang harmony, and they were the same lyrics. It was like two lines of melody moving right on a song sheet, sometimes crossing over each other, and mostly hitting its own parts. Music was strong …it changed everything.

They unrolled the windows in the afternoon light so that the whole world could hear it, and not just them. It was a communal thing, one to be shared desperately with others.

Song after song, they sang to their best ability, their beautiful voices conjoined with each other and spreading elsewhere all around them. They were spreading the fun, the hope, the love.

An hour had passed since the beginning of the car trip, and they were already exhausted from the singing.

"I guess you're right, sometimes you get sick of fun things …" Hazel told him.

Cole merely shrugged.

"Let's have some peace and save the singing for later at the concert …where it's really gonna be turned up a notch," she turned off the music. "And let's just sit in silence."

"Sounds awesome," Cole returned.

The lights of Seattle had started to appear in the distance. They were back to the city-life, though Hazel especially lived more in the immediate suburbs except Cole himself was more in the urban area.

"We're back home! You know that odd feeling when you leave your home for more than a day and then you come back and that's when you get the feeling?" Hazel asked.

"I can relate," Cole said back.

"Good, cuz I get those a lot," she announced.

And then Cole thought about something he hadn't thought about for a long period of time.

The mystery of this parallel reality that once haunted him had no effect anymore. He was free of the bondage, the burden of not knowing. It was certainly an adjustment, but he was over it. Hazel mattered more. Hazel was his universe. And as usual, Hazel couldn't be let down another time after he'd left her the first time.

Who cared about it? He was going to focus on his new life, although it was arguably identical to the one before.

In other words, forget about the past, concentrate on the present and the future.

But yet, there was still that lingering feeling in him that he could return permanently to the reality he'd known all along. There was only one down part he couldn't face, and that was leaving this Hazel. They've been through so much together here and it hurt to go. What made things more complexing was that the Hazel he'd grown up with all his life said that this Hazel here and herself were the same person.

It could all come down to one thing: faith.

Cole needed the faith to believe. But what was faith? Was it blind trust? Was it trusting in something even though there was no evidence or reasoning or anything like that?

If this Hazel was experiencing all this with him, then it meant that the Hazel in the other reality herself was going through the same patterns, and she should therefore recall everything that has happened thus far. Cole didn't want to ponder more; it hurt his internal being.

So many questions and no answers for them. They were floating in the void of darkness of his mind, empty, with not objective and aimless. This dark void was shapeless with no identity and no purpose. It was empty, open-spaced, of no importance, no end. Even space was contained inside, and nothing went beyond this dark void. It was the ultimate place, the place where nothing was.

Cole felt the car start to accelerate up a ramp.

"We're almost there!" Hazel exclaimed exuberantly.

"Can't wait," Cole agreed, although he knew Hazel was way more pumped than he was for this.

"I've waited a long time for this … so," Hazel said.

"Yea," Cole replied.

Cole saw sky beams being projected from a massive hockey stadium in the middle of towering skyscrapers.

"Is that where we are going?" he asked.

"What? That area? Oh yes, my man …that's where we are heading towards," Hazel responded.

Hazel parked in the massive parking lot, and she had to drive several stories up before finding an empty space.

"Only down side for occasions like these is traffic on one hand and a lack of vacant lots," Hazel pointed out.

They hopped out of the car and walked through the sky bridge into the stadium.

Hazel had the two tickets ready and they strode in.

The stadium was circular and it was the home to Seattle's ice hockey team. "Our seats should be 124a and 125a. I think it's over here," Hazel led the way left around the building.

Massive influxes of people were present. Groups of teens all around them were chatting with each other as adolescents their age stood in line to buy food, went to the bathroom or prepared for the concert. There was merchandise with pictures of Andrea Paige on them being sold at $50 and above.

"Here," Hazel let out her hand. Cole followed her onto an opening that had an almost 360 view of the stadium itself. It was huge, gigantic, all the synonyms. So big. Cole's jaw dropped and he gaped at the wide expanse of seats around him and the stage in the middle. People as far away as the eye can see were getting situated in their seats.

They sat rather close to the stage.

"You chose some good seats, thanks Hazel, I really owe this one to you ..." Cole told her.

"You're welcome," Hazel smiled.

Cole and Hazel sat down together, eager for the show to begin.

At last, the people started to flood in quickly and the lights dimmed.

"Now this is cool," Cole complimented.

There was an intro, like the music started and then there was steam billowing up from the stage. And then, the moment everyone had been waiting for arrived.

Andrea Paige skipped out from backstage and started one of her fastest and most popular songs.

Beams of colored light flashed around everywhere and people were jumping and singing the loudest they could.

There could be only one word to sum it all up. It was wild.

Hazel was long gone. She was everywhere. She kept bouncing into Cole and then falling in her seat sometimes as well as hitting the person next to her. Cole was in it very much too.

They were getting hyped. And crazy. And having the most fun they could possibly receive.

Boom! The song ended, and then Andrea said into her mic, "What is up Seattle?" and there was a loud roar.

She sang her next song, a slower and more heart-warming one. Halfway into the song, Cole sneaked a glance at Hazel. Tears were sliding down her face, and her eyes were tearful.

Cole's heart sank for a split-second, but he let her be. It was a very emotional song, and she wasn't alone with the tears. People in every row had tears in their eyes, and even Cole felt an urge to give into the music and lyrics.

The song ended with grandiose. It was splendid.

"You know guys," Andrea spoke. "I've always tried to picture love as something …I tried to see it as an image. But what I've realized after all these years is that you can't contain it. You can't say love is one thing because chances are …it's not. You can't just say oh this is love and this is not love. Love has its own code, it does what it does. You can't make it what you want, but you can certainly act upon it. When you say you do something out of love, you're doing it …but it's really the love that's deciding what effect or impact it has. In sum, just let love be. I know we're humans …we try to shape it to our advantage but sometimes you just gotta let it go. So a word to you guys."

Everyone applauded and cheered. People in their section cried, "Well said" or "So true" or "She's 100% correct." Personally, Cole thought it was true, and judging from Hazel's reaction, she seemed like she agreed wholeheartedly.

Andrea sang her third song. It was amazing.

"With that in mind

All I can do now is dream!

But with you here with me

I can finally rest

No more hardships, no more tests

You'll help me get through the rest

If only we could both run away

It would be like the wind sway"

People started to turn on the flash on their cameras and move their phones side to side in the air. One person started it, and then gradually others followed until the whole stadium was illuminated by the flash lights alone. The music wisped around individuals, winding and bending to connect all the regions together. It was a moment of unity.

Cole poked Hazel in her side and she was like, "Stooooop. Do you want me to do that to you??"

"Not if I get you first," Cole said, and he started poking Hazel from every angle while she attempted to defend herself.

"Stooop. Stoooop. Stop!" she pleaded.

When Cole finally ended, Hazel saw an opportunity and she seized it to get back at him.

Although Cole went haywire, she responded with immense speed.

"Stooop. Stop. Stooppp!" he managed.

"This is revenge for what you did," Hazel explained as she poked him.

"Fine …sorry," Cole replied.

Hazel gave him a few more pokes before she retracted and sat back on her seat.

No one seemed to realize because everyone was dancing and singing, so it wasn't a big scene. Cole scooted closer to Hazel. "It's nice being next to you," Cole told her. "Really?" asked Hazel. "Oh yea, totally," he responded.

She stared at him roundly for a good few seconds.

"What is it?" Cole asked.

"I just like staring at you …got a problem with that?" she retorted.

"No …but it's just normal that people usually don't really stare at other people for so long …" Cole answered.

"You know me …I do things that are real *odd* …" Hazel raised her eyebrows.

"I was about to say that!" Cole responded.

"Honestly, how are we hearing each other when the music's so loud around us?" Hazel blinked. "Are we in a magical trance …like in a circle of ours where sound is muted?" Cole contemplated.

"I hope so …" Hazel replied readily.

"Wait why …?" Cole asked, surprised.

"It's so nice sometimes to take time off and be in a completely different world of your imagination …one where everything is what you want it to be …" Hazel explained.

Then it struck him. Was this a mere fantastical realm where Hazel and he were with each other?

He shook his head, clearing away the idea.

"What's the matter?" Hazel asked, apprehensive.

"Nothing," Cole lied dryly.

Andrea was singing her eighth song by now and the crowd kept dragging the night along.

Sometimes Cole thought about emotions and how it played into one feeling that they missed something. If only he could know everyone in the whole wide world personally …and somehow connect with everybody simultaneously like Andrea was doing …it would be a dream come true. But yet, not everyone was present in the stadium. Other people were probably in other stadiums, cheering on their favorite team, singing in another concert, driving on the road, sleeping, working, having fun elsewhere ...imagine all the possibilities.

And that's what he thought of Hazel.

He couldn't stop looking at her, spending time with her, basically being with her.

And she couldn't do it for him as well.

She couldn't stop looking at him, spending time with him, and really being with him.

The intense link between them dragged on through the rest of the night, apparent in the midst of the dancing crowd, the music, the love being shared with each and every soul in the building.

It was so strong that even after the concert, when everyone was shuffling out, it remained.

This link was there from the moment they'd left the stadium all the way to the point they'd made it back home.

It was so tight that it lasted until they walked through the front door of the house and Archie started licking them.

"Good night Cole," Hazel made a show of waving.

"Good night Hazel," Cole replied, and he trudged up the stairs to his bedroom and collapsed there, falling asleep.

He woke around midnight to take a shower, change, and brush his teeth before going back to bed.

While waiting for his hair to dry, Cole remembered the photograph of Hazel at the roller skating rink in his back pocket and took it out. He took one good glance at it before putting the photograph back. Having time, Cole took a notebook and a pencil and documented all that had happened the days he was there with Hazel …the best days of his life. Whatever happened later on …Cole would never forget.

Outside, it was dark, and unlike the early morning hours, there were no birds chirping or insects buzzing. It was dead silent. He sneaked a peek across the hallway into Hazel's room …no light was on. She was soundly asleep, probably exhausted from the eventful day. Cole smiled. This was how it ought to be. It surely was.

He always longed for that perfect place where things felt so, so good. It wasn't in this world, but he promised himself that one day he would find that place and dwell there for eternity.

There, in the room, he felt the happiest he'd ever felt. It wasn't just because of Hazel, but because of life. All the riches of life had flown through him as though he was liquid water, and he felt like a new person with a new spirit.

Cole didn't want the day to end although it had already did. But time had its own code. He must live the next day now …along with everything it brings. It was nerve-wrecking to think about how it would play out. He wasn't ready …or was he?

And with thoughts floating in his brain, Cole fell into deep sleep.

Hazel wasn't one who gave something up when she set her mind to it but this morning it seemed as if she changed too.

Cole awoke from deep sleep, and the clock read 8:00 dead on. He hurried downstairs as the scent of breakfast appealed to him.

"Good morning!" Hazel cheered, brightened to see him up.

"Hey Hazel, I see you making breakfast …but is it for yourself or for me huh?" Cole joked.

"Uh no and no …it's for both of us," Hazel replied like it was obvious.

Cole sat at the table while she slid the eggs onto two plates and then decorated them with bacon. Then, with careful hands, she walked over with the plates and set them on the table.

"Wow …so conscious…look at u ….already rocking it," Cole complimented as encouragement.

"I prefer to not be careless and clumsy and drop everything …so thank you," Hazel replied.

As Hazel got situated, Cole asked, "So what are we doing today?"

"Oh! I actually crossed everything out and decided to leave them for next time. You were right about too much fun. All we're gonna do is number 13 today, which is the last item on the list...we're going to a place with hills, and we will watch the sunset ...because we missed the sunrise," Hazel responded.

"Dang, we should've woken up early today so we could catch the morning air ...that'd be nice ...but it's ok," Cole answered. "But still ...you didn't have to cross it all out if u didn't want to ...I mean I was just talking so you don't have to take it to heart ..."

"No ...it's fine. I figured it out. It was my decision," Hazel confirmed.

"You go girl ..." Cole replied.

"Yea so we're gonna save the rest for other times ...because can't just have all the fun at once right? And after that ...I'm gonna actually come back here and find a job with the degrees I have ..." Hazel said. "Gotta save some fun for the future ...correct?"

"I agree," Cole agreed.

They enjoyed their breakfast and then headed off from there, hitting the highway once more.

"The place we're going to is really far away …like hours on hours …so hang on," Hazel said.

"Don't worry about me …you focus on driving," Cole responded.

At times, Hazel gunned the engine and sped, believing no cops were around to stop her.

"It's so fun though it's illegal. It's the feeling of being free!" she cried.

"I'm hip," Cole answered, quite intrigued by her boldness.

They passed towns and communities, forests and mountains. It was the world in every aspect being displayed in front of their eyes. All the daily lives. All the people. All the love.

For lunch, they stopped by a fast food area near the exit and continued on from there.

Before sunset, they were driving on a small, dirt road along the countryside and Hazel stopped the car at a certain spot that was completely gorgeous in the sunlight.

She led him atop a hill in the blaring sun and once they got to the top, he could see all the other slopes around him.

Hazel span in a circle, taking it all in, her arms outstretched.

They settled on the hilltop, sitting together crisscrossed. It was the perfect way to end the chapter. It was the perfect way to end the story … a happy ending.

Cole put his arm around Hazel and said in a soft voice, "I love you."

Hazel looked up at him and replied, "I love you too."

Her hair reflected the sunlight, and she was beautiful as ever.

They stared out at the surroundings of nature in its pristine mood.

Cole let loose a breath of air.

The sun was setting now, becoming orange. The streaks of colors appeared in the sky.

Darker was it each minute, but it was also getting prettier by second.

Day was ending, night was coming, the moon shone glamorously.

Little did Cole know this was going to be the last time he would be seeing this …the last time he would be with Hazel. The last moment of his life here had arrived.

But he let it do what it needed to do to him. He let the gush of wind take him away from Hazel …through space and time …back to his home …the reality he'd always known.

Cole remembered it vaguely. Immediately after the wind had blown, he could feel himself losing his grip with Hazel's hand, and then a sudden flashback to the beach.

There he was, on the same beach, on the surfboard, in the same wave. His board skidded across the water as he saw the same images of his life appearing in the walls of water.

The opening at the end was near now. It was there.

I have to go through that, he thought.

It was getting closer by second, and he was about to reappear.

And he zipped out of the wave.

Then darkness. He was falling in dark nothingness with beams of light flying upwards all around him.

Where was he going?

And then he was back. Cole opened his eyes, and he was there on the sand. Back to where he'd started this crazy adventure. Back to the place he'd always known. The real one.

"Hey," a voice said.

Cole darted up and turned slowly, seeing Hazel standing there beside him. "I remember ..." she started.

He didn't get it. He asked her to repeat what she said.

"I remember ... I remember everything. Everything," Hazel told him.

Cole nodded, unsure of how to comprehend things.

"It's okay …I was there …I saw her, I was her. We had a good time together," Hazel continued.

Cole stuttered, his eyes downcast. "Yes …yes we did."

They were speaking to each other like strangers.

And then they were hugging and kissing with tears rolling down their cheeks. The sense of it all was starting to take form. "I saw you …" she whispered in his ear. "I really did."

"Me too," Cole replied softly, his chest growing increasingly rapid from his sobbing. "But I missed you …I missed you so so much."

There, in the sunset, they stood together, next to the ocean.

She squeezed his arm.

"I know it's hard …but remember what I said. If we ever get separated, we'll somehow always be together. We will," she reassured him. "I told you that. I know I did."

"Thanks for being there for me," Cole spoke between tears.

"I will always be there for you, and so will you," she told him.

Acknowledgements

I wrote this book because of all the dreams I'd ever wished to come true. People often tell you to "dream big" or to "imagine your own world" and I fully support those statements. I created this to illustrate my viewpoint of a love story. Most importantly, I wanted to share some life lessons of mine while utilizing rather flirty conversations for your entertainment. Throughout this process, I envisioned many shortcomings for future reference, and I hope you enjoyed the fullest of this book.